THIS BOOK CONTAINS EVERYTHING
YOU ALWAYS KNEW ABOUT

"STAR TREK"

BUT WERE AFRAID NOBODY WOULD ASK!

Like:

the name of the nineteenth-century villian who invades Scotty's body and makes him do all manner of nasty things . . .

the episode in which a group of human-oids attempt to turn the *Enterprise* into a giant refrigerator . . .

the American president who helps Kirk, Spock and Surak square off against four of history's meanest men . . .

Spock's mother's name . . .

What? You don't know?

Better hurry and look inside, and get the facts—and the fun—of a universe of trivia from your favorite TV adventure.

THE OFFICIAL STAR TREK® TRIVIA BOOK

by Trivia Master
Rafe Needleman (Organian)

PUBLISHED BY POCKET BOOKS NEW YORK

To the memory
of my grandmother,
IDA NEEDLEMAN.

Another *Original* publication of POCKET BOOKS

POCKET BOOKS, a Simon & Schuster division of
GULF & WESTERN CORPORATION
1230 Avenue of the Americas, New York, N.Y. 10020

ISBN: 0-671-83090-2

First Pocket Books printing January, 1980

10 9 8 7 6 5 4 3 2 1

POCKET and colophon are trademarks of Simon & Schuster.

Printed in the U.S.A.

Acknowledgments

First, I would like to thank my father for his ideas and help in getting the book published.

I also owe thanks to the following people:

Judy Barkan, whose bionic fingers got this book typed.

My sister Eve, for a few wild and zany ideas along the way.

Joey Canas, for three or four ideas which were too wild to put to paper.

My good friend Duncan Parlett, for help with "The Tholian Web."

And my ninth-grade French teacher, Mrs. Rutherford, who taught me the terribly complicated French needed for the answer to question number 420.

May all of the above live long and prosper.

Contents

Introduction

Among the many needs of this planet, such as a way to feed all humans and the quest for universal peace, lies the need for the ultimate personal "Star Trek" rating system. This ideal system, which has not existed until now, would not discriminate against race, sex, DNA structure, or home planet. To this end I have devoted the past year to writing, as a service to all humanity, *The Official Star Trek Trivia Book*.

This test should only be taken if "Star Trek" has entered into your life and you want either to shove it out or to embed it even more deeply.

From one to five points are awarded for each correct answer, with an occasional ten-pointer. Simply calling them "points" is not sufficient. As we all know, a point occupies neither space nor time, so you cannot measure points. Besides, points are not recognized by Federation High Command. Therefore, after careful deliberation, I have decided to base my quantitative measures not on the *point,* but rather on the " 'Star Trek' Information Gradient"; they will hereafter be referred to simply as "gradients."

The test is based on the honor system, and anyone caught peeking at the answers will be reduced two steps in rank!

At the end of each chapter, you will find a scoring table. Depending upon your score, you will be ranked against certain beings of the galaxy. A score of 75 percent or better will put you up with the super intellect of the Organians, pure energy beings. Below 5 percent lies the Denebian slime devil, a really hideous creature. Somewhere in those ranks, fellow "Star Trek" fan, lies *you!*

I am not including the animated "Star Trek" in this book. Although a good many of the episodes were excellently written and well produced, there were some irreconcilable contradictions with the live-action "Trek." I needn't mention more examples than reel-to-reel tape recorders on the *Enterprise* and *pink* tribbles.

Now, since I am using the titles of the episodes for reference, I am including, in the following pages, a short summary of each episode. It is there only to refresh your memory.

As mentioned earlier, your "Star Trek" intelligence will probably fall somewhere between that of the Organians and the Denebian slime devil. Here are the standards:

Organian	75%–100%
Vulcan	65%– 74%
Talosian	55%– 64%
Human	45%– 54%
Andorian	35%– 44%
Romulan	25%– 34%
Klingon	15%– 24%
Tribble	5%– 14%
Denebian slime devil	0%– 4%

And as you make your way through these intergalactic pages, remember the immortal words of Kahless the Unforgettable: "It matters not whether you win or lose, as long as you do better than your friends."

Rafe Needleman

Plot Summaries

"ALL OUR YESTERDAYS": Kirk, Spock, and McCoy find themselves in different pasts on a planet whose sun is about to go nova.

"THE ALTERNATIVE FACTOR": Rivals from two parallel, negative universes attempt to destroy each other. If they both emerge in the same universe, both universes will be annihilated.

"AMOK TIME": Following a seven-year cycle, Spock must return to Vulcan and find a mate, or die.

"AND THE CHILDREN SHALL LEAD": The United Federation of Planets is threatened by a group of children (under the spell of the evil "Gorgan"), who use people's inner fears to bring out the worst in them.

"THE APPLE": The *Enterprise* is held captive by the super-machine/god "Vaal," who rules a planet of humanoids, making them docile and non-productive.

"ARENA": The "Gorns" destroy a remote starbase, and the "Metrons" stage a battle between Kirk and the Gorn captain to decide who keeps the planet.

"ASSIGNMENT: EARTH": Returning to 1968 Earth (on purpose), the *Enterprise* contacts Gary Seven, a human from an advanced civilization, who is trying to help Earth survive. But, in a critical moment, Kirk doubts Seven's goodwill.

"BALANCE OF TERROR": A Romulan "bird of prey" ship enters Federation territory with a new super-weapon. The Romulans and the *Enterprise* battle it out. (This was the first time Romulans were shown.)

"BREAD AND CIRCUSES": A landing party of Kirk, Spock, and McCoy beams down to a planet where Rome never fell. Former spaceship captain Merrick is on the planet and has broken the Prime Directive. (The Prime Directive states: "You shall not interfere with a developing culture.")

"BY ANY OTHER NAME": Alien invaders from the Andromeda galaxy hijack the *Enterprise* for a journey "home." They are eventually corrupted by the human form they took to use the *Enterprise*.

"CATSPAW": Kirk and a landing party discover a planet with ghosts, goblins, and a haunted mansion. They are then abducted by two resident sorcerers, Korob and Sylvia.

"THE CHANGELING": Nomad, a super-robot/computer, is beamed aboard the *Enterprise*. The crew discovers a little late that Nomad's purpose is to sterilize (destroy) life forms that are not "perfect" by its own standards.

"CHARLIE X": Charlie Evans, a seventeen-year-old boy alone since birth, is aboard the *Enterprise* when it is discovered that he has been given super-powers by the "Thasians" and cannot live in society without endangering others.

"THE CITY ON THE EDGE OF FOREVER": McCoy, under influence of a drug, goes back into 1930 Earth through the Guardian of Forever. He meets Edith Keeler and changes history so the Federation never existed. Kirk and Spock must right what he did wrong, or face a life of loneliness on a barren planet.

"THE CLOUD MINDERS": On a strange planet with a floating cloud city, Kirk is drawn into a class struggle when he tries to obtain zienite, the only known antidote to a botanical plague.

"THE CONSCIENCE OF THE KING": Koridian, star of a group of traveling actors, may be the infamous executioner "Kodos." Trying to find the truth, Kirk almost gets himself killed.

"THE CORBOMITE MANEUVER": The *Enterprise* is threatened by a small humanoid called "Balok," who has at his disposal a gigantic and powerful starship.

"COURT-MARTIAL": Kirk is accused of murdering a crewman, Finney, who has altered the ship's computers to present damaging evidence to Kirk.

"DAGGER OF THE MIND": Dr. Van Gelder, deranged escapee from a penal colony, causes Kirk to investigate. Kirk discovers a lethal "mind drainer" which eventually kills the colony's warden.

"DAY OF THE DOVE": A non-corporeal being which feeds on hatred invades the minds of the *Enterprise* crew and those of a Klingon ship, causing them to battle ruthlessly, while the *Enterprise* is heading toward the galaxy's edge.

"THE DEADLY YEARS": Kirk and a landing party beam down to a planet, only to find they are aging supernormally when they return.

"THE DEVIL IN THE DARK": Replying to a distress call from a mining colony, the *Enterprise* crew discovers a creature capable of moving through solid rock—the "Horta." The colony workers are sure it must be destroyed until they find out it's only a mother protecting her eggs.

"THE DOOMSDAY MACHINE": Kirk must stop a milelong, cigar-shaped planet killer before it reaches the heart of the United Federation. If this is not enough, he also has to contend with Matt Decker, disturbed captain of one of the *Enterprise*'s sister ships, the *Constellation*.

"ELAAN OF TROYIUS": The *Enterprise* is assigned to transport Elaan, warrior ruler, from one planet to an enemy planet, where Elaan is to be married to the enemy's ruler. En route it is discovered that she is too savage for the other planet, and must be taught new manners.

"THE EMPATH": On a dying planet, Kirk, Spock, and McCoy stumble across "Gem," a mute telepath who is able to heal others with her mind, and two robed aliens who subject Kirk and McCoy to senseless tortures.

"THE ENEMY WITHIN": A "Jekyll and Hyde" story. A malfunctioning transporter splits Kirk into two people, one good and one evil.

"THE *Enterprise* INCIDENT": Kirk, in trying to steal the Romulan invisibility machine, is captured and charged with espionage. Meanwhile, the beautiful Romulan commander is trying to woo Spock to the Romulans' side.

"ERRAND OF MERCY": A war is brewing between the Federation of Planets and the Klingon Empire. Kirk, as a gesture of good faith, offers protection to the primitive inhabitants of a disputed planet. But it turns out the inhabitants are super-advanced, pure-energy beings who eventually stop the war that almost started.

"FOR THE WORLD IS HOLLOW AND I HAVE TOUCHED THE SKY": McCoy contracts a fatal illness, giving him a year to live. The *Enterprise* crew discovers a wandering spaceship-asteroid whose inhabitants are the descendants of the now extinct "Fabrini." The oracle of the asteroid (a computer) leads the people to believe they are on a planet, not a spaceship.

"FRIDAY'S CHILD": The Feds and Klingons are fighting for mining rights on the planet Capella. Kirk violates a tribal custom (he touches the "Teer's" wife, Eleen), and he, Spock, and McCoy must flee to the hills with Eleen, nine months pregnant.

"THE *Galileo Seven*": The shuttlecraft *Galileo*, Spock in command, is forced to land on a hostile planet. They must lift off and catch the *Enterprise* before it leaves, or fall prey to eight-foot-tall, woolly natives.

"THE GAMESTERS OF TRISKELION": Kirk, Uhura, and Chekov are whisked to a planet where they find themselves in "collars of obedience" (pain-giving devices), and are forced to fight with aliens to amuse their masters—bodiless minds.

"THE IMMUNITY SYNDROME": The *Enterprise* finds a gargantuan single cell wandering through space. Spock volunteers to enter the cell in the shuttlecraft and appears lost. It's discovered that the thing is about to reproduce, and the *Enterprise* must destroy it, or perish.

"I, MUDD": An android, Norman, takes over the *Enterprise*, and brings it to Harry Mudd, ruler of a whole society of androids. But, just as Mudd is leaving, the androids revolt, trapping Mudd on his "paradise."

"IS THERE IN TRUTH NO BEAUTY?": An alien, so ugly the sight of him will drive a human (or Vulcan) insane, is beamed aboard with a blind telepath, Miranda. Miranda becomes jealous of Spock's pure telepathy, and when Spock catches a glimpse of the alien, Miranda (who can heal the insanity) has doubts about saving Spock.

"JOURNEY TO BABEL": The *Enterprise* takes on ambassadors from many planets, including Sarek and Amanda, Spock's parents. Sarek has the equivalent of a heart attack and desperately needs blood only Spock can give. But Spock feels his duty to the *Enterprise* is more important.

"LET THAT BE YOUR LAST BATTLEFIELD": Two strange aliens (white on one side, black on the other) try to resolve a centuries'-old war on the *Enterprise,* not knowing the war has killed their civilization.

"THE LIGHTS OF ZETAR": Scotty finds true love with Mira Romaine, even though a strange electrical being has invaded her mind and is threatening her life.

"THE MAN TRAP": A mysterious salt-sucking creature, with ability to change its appearance, threatens the *Enterprise* crew.

"MARK OF GIDEON": Kirk is decoyed onto a duplicate, stationary *Enterprise,* while Spock racks his brain trying to figure out where Kirk is. Meanwhile, the Gideonites need Kirk for selfish medical reasons.

"THE MENAGERIE" (I & II): The only two-part "Star Trek" episode. Spock hijacks the *Enterprise* to the forbidden planet of Talos IV, where former Captain Pike's encounter with the inhabitants is displayed.

"METAMORPHOSIS": The shuttlecraft is forced to land on an alien planet by a hydrogen-ion cloud. It turns out that the cloud is a presumed-dead man's "companion."

"MIRI": Discovering an identical Earth, a landing party beams down only to find 300-year-old children with long-dead parents.

"MIRROR, MIRROR": During an ion storm, Kirk, Mc-

Coy, Uhura, Scotty, and Chekov beam into an alternate universe where the Federation is a Klingon-like organization and the ship's computer has a male voice.

"MUDD'S WOMEN": Con man Harry Mudd transports onto the *Enterprise* with three irresistible women and a strange "Venus drug." He also manages to burn out the *Enterprise*'s engines.

"THE NAKED TIME": An *Enterprise* crewman beams up from a frozen planet carrying a water-borne virus. Lieutenant Riley takes over the engine room and nearly succeeds in destroying the starship.

"OBSESSION": Kirk becomes obsessed with killing a gaseous blood-sucking monster, a monster that theoretically cannot exist. He puts the *Enterprise* and his own command in danger.

"THE OMEGA GLORY": The deranged Captain Tracy believes he has found immortality on the planet Omega. He kills his crew and violates the Prime Directive by using his phaser to kill the primitive "Yangs," enemies of his friends, the "Kohms."

"OPERATION: ANNIHILATE!": Mysterious blob-like, flying creatures that attack the spinal cord invade an Earth colony, killing Kirk's only brother. They must be stopped, lest they spread to Earth.

"THE PARADISE SYNDROME": On a mercy mission, Kirk trips into an obelisk and contracts amnesia. He then falls in love with an Indian girl of the planet. Spock must once again rack his brains to find Kirk, in addition to saving the planet, which is about to be smashed by an asteroid.

"PATTERNS OF FORCE": The *Enterprise* warps its way into a star system with two inhabited planets, Zeon and Ekos. In this system, Ekos is a Nazi culture, and the Zeons are the scapegoats.

"A PIECE OF THE ACTION": In this comedy, Kirk gets kidnapped by gangsters, walks on a pool table, and drives a Ford. Spock says, "I'd advise yahs ta keep dialin'," and McCoy wields a machine gun.

"PLATO'S STEPCHILDREN": Human-appearing beings with telekinetic abilities and selfish desires try to imprison Kirk, Spock, and McCoy. The dwarf Alexander is their clue to freedom.

"A PRIVATE LITTLE WAR": The natives of a primitive planet get guns from Klingons. Kirk must supply firearms to the opposition, although it violates the Prime Directive.

"REQUIEM FOR METHUSELAH": Kirk's landing party invades the private paradise of an immortal man. Kirk falls in love (again) with Reena, android creation and heartthrob of this undying man.

"THE RETURN OF THE ARCHONS": While searching for a lost starship (the *Archon*), the *Enterprise* crew discovers a culture where the people are ruled by a computer which manages to keep them peaceful and zombie-like.

"RETURN TO TOMORROW": Alien super-intelligences

have their entities transplanted into select *Enterprise* officers. All is going well until the entity in Spock decides it wants to keep the body for its own—which means the death of Spock.

"THE SAVAGE CURTAIN": An alien rock-creature, seeking the meaning of good and evil, forces Kirk, Spock, Surak, and President Lincoln to do battle with four of history's meanest men.

"SHORE LEAVE": While trying to get some rest and recreation on a beautiful planet, the *Enterprise* crew is inundated with dreams-come-true, such as white rabbits, tigers, and Samurai warriors.

"SPACE SEED": The *Enterprise* intercepts a 200-year-old "sleeper ship" full of people in suspended animation. Their captain, Khan, almost succeeds in taking over the *Enterprise* as a prelude to conquering the universe.

"SPECTRE OF THE GUN": For violating Melkotian space, Kirk, Spock, and McCoy are forced into a staged gunfight at the O.K. Corral, where they play the part of the Clantons, the historical losers.

"SPOCK'S BRAIN": An alien woman boards the *Enterprise* and swipes Spock's mind to use it as the "controller" of an underground habitat. The brain must be found, or Spock's complex body will die without it.

"THE SQUIRE OF GOTHOS": Kirk and party are held captive on an uncharted planet by an omnipotent (almost) being called Trelane. It turns out that Trelane is an immature alien child who is fascinated with his human and Vulcan playthings.

"A TASTE OF ARMAGEDDON": Kirk must play diplomat and stop a 500-year-old war between two planets that is being fought cleanly and efficiently with computers.

"THAT WHICH SURVIVES": A landing party from the *Enterprise* gets itself stranded on a barren planet and then has to contend with a computer-produced woman whose touch causes instant death.

"THIS SIDE OF PARADISE": Kirk's crew leaves in a huff for a planet where spore-producing plants give all who come near them a natural high. Kirk, feeling regretful and stubborn, does not succumb to the plants.

"THE THOLIAN WEB": The *Enterprise* discovers one of her sister ships drifting in a region of space that causes men to go mad. Kirk vanishes to another universe, and, while Spock tries to rescue him, the *Enterprise* is attacked by not-so-friendly aliens.

"TOMORROW IS YESTERDAY": Our favorite starship is swept into Earth's 1960s. Before returning to his own century, however, Kirk must erase all traces of the *Enterprise* having been there, or risk altering history.

"THE TROUBLE WITH TRIBBLES": A classic. Living fuzz-balls that purr invade the *Enterprise* and a space station. These little tribbles multiply, and must be disposed of (humanely). The only problem is—everyone loves them.

"TURNABOUT INTRUDER": "Star Trek's" last TV episode. A crazed woman finds a contraption that moves people's souls. She puts hers in Kirk's body and Kirk's being in hers.

"THE ULTIMATE COMPUTER": A super-computer is installed on the *Enterprise*. When it starts mercilessly zapping cargo vessels and starships, it is discovered that the "off" switch does not work.

"THE WAY TO EDEN": The *Enterprise* captures six "space hippies," who are searching for paradise in the form of a planet named Eden. The problem with this Eden, though, is that all of its foliage contains a powerful acid which both burns skin and is a deadly poison.

"WHAT ARE LITTLE GIRLS MADE OF?": On an icy planet, Kirk finds the presumed-dead scientist Dr. Corby. Kirk finds out that all of Dr. Corby's helpers are androids. He later discovers that Dr. Corby himself is not a human anymore, but a human mind in an android body.

"WHERE NO MAN HAS GONE BEFORE": In this episode, the *Enterprise* travels beyond the galaxy's edge. Two crew members get transformed into "superior" beings, and Kirk nearly meets his maker in trying to stop them from doing evil deeds.

"WHOM GODS DESTROY": Spock and Kirk are taken captive by an insane man who has acquired the ability to change his appearance to that of anyone else. This man, once a prisoner in an insane asylum, now ruler of the same, is scheming to take over the galaxy.

"WHO MOURNS FOR ADONIS?": An *Enterprise* landing

party is taken captive by a being who calls himself the god Apollo. He wants Kirk's crew to worship him and behave like lambs.

"WINK OF AN EYE": A group of humanoids, who live at a super-accelerated rate, attempt to seize the *Enterprise* and turn it into a giant refrigerator. In this way, they hope to use the crew of the *Enterprise* to continue their species.

"WOLF IN THE FOLD": The spirit of Jack the Ripper runs rampant aboard the *Enterprise* feeding on a unique diet of one human emotion—fear.

1.

What planet is this?
   a. Earth
   b. Rigel VII
   c. Vega XI
   d. Arskannojle-Flosbleskur
(3)

chapter one

SPACE STATIONS, STARS, GALAXIES, AND ENTIRE CIVILIZATIONS

2. "Berthold rays" bombard which planet of the Federation?
   (3)

3. In what quadrant is the planet Gothos? ("The Squire of Gothos")
   (5)

4. Who are the two peoples of the planet in "A Private Little War"?
   (3)

5. What was a merciful form of execution on Vulcan in ancient times? ("Journey to Babel")
   (2)

6. In "The Trouble with Tribbles," what is being protected in the space station's storage compartment?
   (1)

7. Where are the Scalosians rated on the industrial scale? ("Wink of an Eye") (4)

8. How old is the planet in "That Which Survives"? (5)

9. In what star system is the planet in the episode "Bread and Circuses"? (5)

10. In "A Piece of the Action," what is the name of the company that makes "the sweetest little automatic in the world"? (5)

11. According to "Wolf in the Fold," how long ago was the "great awakening" of the planet Argelius? (4)

12. What type of planet (A, B, M, Z, etc.) is Planet Mudd? ("I, Mudd") (5)

13. According to "The Changeling," how many people are in the Malurian system? (4)

14. In what episode is Organia the main planet? (3)

15. What does "Landru" mean to the inhabitants of Beta III? (1)

16. What is the name of the space station in "The Trouble with Tribbles"?
(1)

17. Of what planet is Chief Vanderberg security head?
(4)

18. What is the starbase in "Court-Martial"?
(4)

19. In "The *Galileo Seven*" the *Enterprise* has to reach a particular planet to stop a plague. What is the planet?
(4)

20. From what planet is Eve McHuron? ("Mudd's Women")
(5)

21. What was Mudd's original destination in "Mudd's Women"?
(5)

22. Where was Harry Mudd born? ("Mudd's Women")
(10)

23. Where are Charlie's closest living relatives? ("Charlie X")
(5)

24. What's so special about the planet known as Ardana?
(3)

25. In what episode do Troglytes appear and what planet are they from?
(3)

26. In "Amok Time," toward what planet was the *Enterprise* heading before it was diverted to Vulcan?
(5)

27. In the beginning of "The Immunity Syndrome," what starbase is the *Enterprise* approaching?
(5)

28. In which episode is the United Earth Space Probe Agency mentioned?
(5)

29. Where is the planet in "Errand of Mercy" rated on the Richter scale of cultures?
(5)

30. What is the main output of the mining colony of Janus VI? ("The Devil in the Dark")
(4)

31. On what planet is the penal colony in "Dagger of the Mind"?
(4)

32. Where is "fizzbin" played? ("A Piece of the Action")
(2)

33. In "By Any Other Name," where did Scotty get the alcoholic beverage he refers to as "Green"?
(5)

34.

Which episode?
(5)

35. Which solar system's star is about to go nova in "The Empath"?
(4)

36. Why is it unlikely that the planet in "The Paradise Syndrome" still exists?
(4)

37. In the twenty-third century, Earth's sun is commonly called ———. (It is now, too, but not as commonly.)
(2)

38. What solar system did the amoeba of "The Immunity Syndrome" destroy?
(4)

39. Before the U.S.S. *Horizon* contaminated the planet in "A Piece of the Action," what was the state of the planet's culture?
(3)

40. Most of the action in "The Man Trap" takes place on which planet?
(3)

41. If you were reading a magazine called *The Gallian,* what planet would you most likely be on?
(5)

42. What is the home planet of the androids of the Old Ones? ("What Are Little Girls Made Of?")
(3)

43. What is the inner planet in the Tellun star system? (10)

44. In "And the Children Shall Lead," to what planet do the kiddies want to go? (4)

45. From what planet is Rojan? ("By Any Other Name") (5)

46. What are the two planets in the M43 Alpha system? (5)

47. How many suns does Triskelion of "The Gamesters of Triskelion" have? (2)

48. What is the penalty for fraud on Deneb V? ("I, Mudd") (2)

49. What is the planet affected by madness in "Operation: Annhilate!"? (2)

50. In "A Taste of Armageddon," with whom is Eminiar VII at war? (4)

51. Does Vulcan have any moons? (2)

52. What planet did the U.S.S. *Horizon* contaminate? ("A Piece of the Action")
(4)

53. Where did Janice Lester find the life-entity transfer machine? (That's a machine that puts one person's soul in another's body and vice versa.)
(5)

54. On what planet was the Starnes expedition conducted?
(2)

55. What is the population of Daran V? (Daran V is the planet that would have been smashed to bits by the spaceship/asteroid called Yonada if the *Enterprise* hadn't stopped it.) ("For the World Is Hollow and I Have Touched the Sky")
(5)

56. What is the Platonians' home star in "Plato's Stepchildren"?
(10)

57. If the *Enterprise* hadn't stopped the planet killer in "The Doomsday Machine," which would have been the next system to go?
(4)

58. From what planet is Ambassador Petri?
(3)

59. Approximately how many planets are in the Federation? ("Metamorphosis")
(4)

60. How many planets are destroyed in "The Doomsday Machine"?
    (5)

61. In "The Devil in the Dark," on which level are the silicon nodules discovered?
    (5)

62. What planet is Gary Seven from? ("Assignment: Earth")
    (2)

63.

In which episode is Sulu convinced that he is an eighteenth-century swordsman?
(2)

chapter two

DECISIONS, DECISIONS . . .

64. What is Tharn's reason for not giving the Federation his planet's dilithium crystals? (Tharn is leader of the Halkan Council in "Mirror, Mirror.")
    (3)

65. In which episode is Scotty ready to "nurse" his warp engines?
    (4)

66. In "The *Enterprise* Incident," what is Kirk's excuse for entering Romulan territory?
    (4)

67. According to "Bread and Circuses," why was Merrick dropped from the Space Academy?
    (4)

68. When does Kirk fire Scotty from his job?
    (2)

69. In "Obsession," what tape does Nurse Chapel use to get Ensign Garrovick to eat?
(3)

70. In "Journey to Babel," what was the issue facing the delegates on the *Enterprise?*
(2)

71. In "Catspaw," how does Korob try to bribe Kirk, Spock, and McCoy?
(3)

72. Why did Matt Decker kill himself? ("The Doomsday Machine")
(1)

73. In "Amok Time," who is T'Pring's "champion"?
(1)

74. What was the most difficult decision of Kirk's life (*not* his career)?
(5)

75. What does Kirk think of hobbies? ("The City on the Edge of Forever")
(2)

76. How do the Organians prevent the Federation and the Klingons from fighting?
(2)

77. In "Day of the Dove," who is first to order a "cease hostilities," Kang or Kirk?
(2)

78. Whom does Kirk put in charge of Spock when Spock is under arrest in "This Side of Paradise"? (4)

79. In "Journey to Babel," does Sarek favor admission of Coridan? (1)

80. What does Spock suggest to scare off the creatures in "The *Galileo Seven*"? (3)

81. When McCoy has to beam up to the *Enterprise* in the beginning of Act I of "The Menagerie I," why does he think he is being called? (3)

82. In "The Corbomite Maneuver," what does Spock suggest that Navigator Bailey have removed? (3)

83. In "The Corbomite Maneuver," what does Navigator Bailey "vote" that Kirk do to the cube? (2)

84. Why does Van Gelder come aboard the *Enterterprise* in "Dagger of the Mind"? (3)

85. What is the first thought that Dr. Noel puts into Kirk's mind? ("Dagger of the Mind") (4)

86. In "The *Galileo Seven*," why does Spock jettison the fuel of the shuttlecraft?
(2)

87. Where does Miri try to hide from the *Enterprise* landing party? ("Miri")
(3)

88. According to "What Are Little Girls Made Of?", Nurse Chapel gave up a career in what field to sign on the *Enterprise?*
(5)

89. In "Mudd's Women," what does Kirk charge Mudd with?
(5)

90. When Kirk realizes he has a double on board (in "The Enemy Within"), he orders all security men's phasers to be locked on force setting —————.
(4)

91. If Kirk were eluding a mass search, where would he go? ("The Enemy Within")
(3)

92. How does Khan like McGiver's hair? ("Space Seed")
(3)

93. In "The Trouble with Tribbles," how many Klingons does Kirk tell Koloth he will allow to *beam over* to the space station? (Watch out; this one is tricky.)
(5)

94. In "The Immunity Syndrome," whom does Kirk "condemn to death" by letting him use the shuttle-craft to penetrate the amoeba?
    (1)

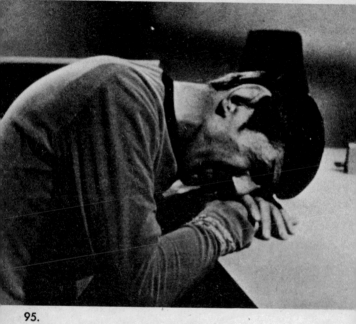

95.

What's wrong with Spock?
(4)

chapter three

SPOCKOLOGY

96. In the Vulcan marriage ceremony, which is used first, the ahn-woon or the lirpa? ("Amok Time") (4)

97. In "The Trouble with Tribbles," does Spock know what quadrotriticale is? (1)

98. Are the Vulcans an offshoot of the Romulans? (4)

99. Why is Spock's blood green? (3)

100. What is Spock's blood type? (3)

101. What is the name of Spock's mother? (1)

102.

Only once does Spock appear wearing a beard. Under what conditions?
  a. First Officer in an alternate universe
  b. engineer of the *Enterprise* under Captain Pike
  c. in his future, revealed by the Guardian of Forever
  d. in his first appearance on "Star Trek," before changes were made

(1)

103. Spock mans what station on the bridge of the *Enterprise*?
     (1)

104. What is the Vulcan death grip?
     (2)

105. When does Spock wear the Vulcan IDIC?
     (2)

106. What is Spock's computer classification? ("The Ultimate Computer")
(5)

107. Where is Spock's heart?
(3)

108. What is Spock's serial number?
(10)

109. What is the physical range of Vulcan telepathy?
(5)

110. In which episode is it stated that "Vulcans never bluff"?
(2)

111. What is "All" in the Vulcan philosophy? ("The Savage Curtain")
(4)

112. According to "Amok Time," what is the Vulcan word for "time of mating"?
(2)

113. How long has Spock been in Star Fleet?
(3)

114. "On that day I shall mourn." Which day is Spock referring to?
(4)

115. In "Journey to Babel," how old is Spock's father?
(3)

116. Spock reminds Apollo of—whom? ("Who Mourns for Adonis?")
    (3)

117. What animals does Spock compare himself with in "Amok Time"?
    (2)

118. The Vulcan mating drive comes every ——— years.
    (1)

119.
The mental state Spock has entered here is known as Plak tow. What English term is used to characterize this state in "Amok Time"?
(2)

120.
Why is this man smiling?
(3)

121. In "Errand of Mercy," whom does Spock masquerade as so that the Klingons will not be suspicious?
(3)

122. In "This Side of Paradise," what does Spock see in a cloud formation that reminds him of a certain creature on Berengaria VII?
(5)

123. What reference does Kirk make to Spock's childhood in "The Squire of Gothos" that would be absolutely out of place in the *Enterprise*'s time period?
(4)

124. In which episode does Spock admit to being stubborn?
(3)

125. Do Vulcans drink alcoholic beverages?
(2)

126. What is the first episode in which Spock uses the Vulcan mind meld?
(5)

127. What is Spock's pulse and blood pressure near the beginning of "The Naked Time"?
(10)

128. Before Sarek retired, to how many planets was he ambassador? ("Journey to Babel")
(5)

129. Are Spock's legs ever broken? If so, in what episode?
(2)

130. Who calls Spock "Mister Ears," and in which episode?
(3)

131. Why are Vulcans' ears larger than those of Earthlings, and why are they pointed?
(5)

132.

The one and only Captain James T. Kirk.
   a. What is his serial number?
(10)
   b. In what episode are his ears as pointed as Spock's,
      and why?
(2)

chapter four

SPACE PEOPLE

133. How many episodes does Yeoman Janice Rand appear in?
(5)

134. How many live-action "Star Trek" episodes has Harry Mudd appeared in?
(1)

135. What are the names of the two people who are getting married in "Balance of Terror"?
(4)

136. Where was Lieutenant Kevin Riley born? ("The Conscience of the King")
(10)

137. Who is the one Terran who doesn't remind Korax (a Klingon) of Regulan blood worms? ("The Trouble with Tribbles")
(2)

138. Why is Salish, Indian medicine chief of "The Paradise Syndrome," ignorant of the secrets of the meteor-deflecting obelisk?
    (3)

139. Who is Melakon?
    (3)

140. How old is Roberta Lincoln? ("Assignment: Earth")
    (4)

141. Who was Jamie Finney named after?
    (2)

142. Who is "First Citizen" on planet 892-IV? ("Bread and Circuses")
    (2)

143. "Garth of ————"?
    (3)

144. What is Lieutenant Kelso's first name? ("Where No Man Has Gone Before")
    (3)

145. Give the names of *at least four* awards Kirk has received. ("Court-Martial")
    (5)

146. Which of the "Star Trek" characters is an admirer of Abraham Lincoln?
    (2)

147.

There is one epidermal (look it up) feature that distinguishes the mirror universe Sulu from our Sulu. What is it? ("Mirror, Mirror")
(4)

148. Who is the head of Sector 9 of Star Fleet Command? ("Amok Time")
(10)

149. Who is the "Captain's Woman" in "Mirror, Mirror"?
(3)

150. In which episode does a barbershop appear?
(5)

151. Who was chief surgeon of the *Enterprise* when Christopher Pike was in command?
(5)

152. In "The Menagerie I," how old is Vina said to be when discovered by the *Enterprise* crew?
(3)

153. In reality, who is Ivan Burkoff? ("The Trouble with Tribbles")
(4)

154. What is the purpose of Mudd's journey in "Mudd's Women"?
(4)

155. Which person from "Star Trek" was born on Martian Colony #3?
(5)

156. Who is the governor of Elba II? ("Whom Gods Destroy")
(4)

157. According to "Day of the Dove," who is Chekov's brother?
(2)

158. Which one of the designers of the *Enterprise* do we see in "Is There in Truth No Beauty?"?
(4)

159. Who is the "spokesperson" for the group of children in "And the Children Shall Lead"?
(4)

160. What do the Indian people call Kirk in "This Side of Paradise"?
(2)

161. Who is Gary Seven's secretary in "Assignment: Earth"?
(2)

162. In "Bread and Circuses," who is the "last of the barbarians"?
(3)

163. In which episode does Commodore Enwright appear?
(4)

164. Who designed the computers on the *Enterprise?*
(2)

165. Who is the captain of the *Exeter* in "The Omega Glory"?
(4)

166. Who was Kirk's instructor at the Space Academy? ("Patterns of Force")
(5)

167. In "Wolf in the Fold," who caused the explosion that threw Scotty against a bulkhead?
(3)

168. In "Wolf in the Fold," where is Mr. Hengist from?
(3)

169. Who is the security duty officer in "Obsession"?
(4)

170. How much younger is Lieutenant Gallway than Kirk in "The Deadly Years"?
(4)

171. Who is the desk-bound paper-pusher in "The Deadly Years" who commands the *Enterprise* right through Romulan territory?
(4)

172. In "Metamorphosis," what is Nancy Hedford's mission?
(3)

173. For what is Zefrem Cochrane famous?
(1)

174. Who was in Uhura's place in "The Doomsday Machine"?
(4)

175. What is Matt Decker's rank? ("The Doomsday Machine")
(2)

176. In "Mirror, Mirror," which members of the landing party find their universe shifted?
(3)

177. According to "The Changeling," who created Nomad?
(3)

178. In "Who Mourns for Adonis?", who is Scotty's lady friend?
    (4)

179. After Spock and Chekov, who takes over the library-computer station?
    (4)

180. In "Charlie X," what does Charlie think Yeoman Rand's favorite color is?
    (2)

181. How old is Kirk?
    (4)

182. How old is Chekov in "Who Mourns for Adonis?"?
    (4)

183. Who is "Sam" and where does he live?
    (2)

184. In "Shore Leave," who is Kirk's long-lost love?
    (3)

185. In "The City on the Edge of Forever," of what is Edith Keeler the director?
    (2)

186. In "The City on the Edge of Forever," who calls Miss Keeler "Miss Goody Two-Shoes"?
    (3)

187. Commodore Barstow appears in which episode?
    (5)

188. Who is the first colonist seen by the *Enterprise* crew on the planet in "This Side of Paradise"? (3)

189. In "This Side of Paradise," which *Enterprise* crew member states that he was born in Mojave? (5)

190. What is Anan 7's full name? ("A Taste of Armageddon") (4)

191. In "Court-Martial," who is Kirk's defending attorney? And whom does he defend after Kirk? (3)

192. In "Court-Martial," what is Benjamin Finney's job (or rank)? (4)

193. Who "doesn't believe in little green men"—until he sees Spock in "Tomorrow Is Yesterday"? (1)

194. In "Tomorrow Is Yesterday," who are the first two people from the *Enterprise* to beam down to Earth? (2)

195. In "The Squire of Gothos," who are the first two people to disappear from the *Enterprise?* (3)

196. Galactic High Commissioner Ferris is in what episode? (4)

197. In "Shore Leave," who first compares the planet to something from *Alice in Wonderland?*
(1)

198. In "Shore Leave," which crew member's reaction time is down 9 to 12 percent?
(2)

199. Who was Kirk's "personal devil" at the Space Academy? ("Shore Leave")
(2)

200. What is the disguise of Kodos, the executioner, in "The Conscience of the King"?
(2)

201. According to "The Conscience of the King," who is the captain of the *Astral Queen?*
(5)

202. Who are the only two people on the *Enterprise* who ever saw Kodos? ("The Conscience of the King")
(4)

203. In "The Corbomite Maneuver," for what reason is Kirk in sick bay?
(3)

204. What color is Kirk's shirt at the beginning of "I, Mudd"? (If you don't have a color TV, which of his shirts is it?)
(5)

205. Who is Kirk's girl in "The Deadly Years"?
(3)

206. What is Dr. Adams's first name? ("Dagger of the Mind")
(2)

207. In "Dagger of the Mind," with whom does Kirk beam down to the planet?
(4)

208. In "Miri," who is the first member of the Enterprise crew to get the disease?
(4)

209. What is Dr. Korby's first name? ("What Are Little Girls Made Of?")
(2)

210. What is Nurse Chapel's first name?
(1)

211. In the game of 3-D chess between Kirk and Spock in "Charlie X," who wins?
(2)

212. In "Mudd's Women," how many brothers does Eve have?
(4)

213. In "Mudd's Women," what are the names of all three of the miners on Rigel XII?
(10)

214. What does Harry Mudd say his name is in "Mudd's Women"?
   (2)

215. What were Mudd's past offenses? ("Mudd's Women")
   (4)

216. What is Mudd's full name?
   (1)

217. What are the names of all of "Mudd's Women," in the episode of the same name?
   (5)

218. Who is in the navigator's position at the beginning of "Mudd's Women"?
   (4)

219. Name the crewman who transports up and contaminates the transporter in "The Enemy Within."
   (3)

220. What drink does Kirk's double (the evil one) crave in "The Enemy Within"?
   (2)

221. In "The Naked Time," what is Sulu's hobby?
   (1)

222. In "The Naked Time," who are the first people from the *Enterprise* to beam down to the planet?
   (4)

223. In "Charlie X," what is the name of the navigator on the *Antares?*
     (4)

224. In "Charlie X," what is Charlie's full name?
     (1)

225. Who was the first girl Charlie ever saw? ("Charlie X")
     (2)

226. How does McCoy describe Charlie (medically) in "Charlie X"?
     (2)

227. How close did Nurse Chapel and Dr. Korby come to being married? ("What Are Little Girls Made Of?")
     (3)

228. What is the name of the girl Janice Rand is fixing Charlie up with in "Charlie X"?
     (4)

229. In "The Man Trap," how many humans are on the planet when the *Enterprise* lands?
     (2)

230. In "The Man Trap," why and to whom is Janice Rand carrying the tray of food?
     (4)

231. What does Kirk call himself while he is masquerading as an Organian in "Errand of Mercy"?
     (3)

232. From what star system is Zefrem Cochrane? ("Metamorphosis") (10)

233. What is McCoy's first name? (1)

234. In "Who Mourns for Adonis?", what does "A-and-A officer" stand for? (3)

235. Which member of the *Enterprise* crew buys the first tribble? ("The Trouble with Tribbles") (4)

236. Who is the commander of Space Station K-7? ("The Trouble with Tribbles") (2)

237. What is the name and rank of the historian who specializes in the late twentieth century in "Space Seed"? (2)

238. Who is Kirk's lady friend who later acts as a lawyer *against* him in "Court-Martial"? (4)

239. In "The Trouble with Tribbles," when Kirk wants a chicken sandwich and coffee, why can't he have it? (1)

240. Was Garth ever a starship captain? ("Whom Gods Destroy")
(3)

241. How much of the *Enterprise*'s complement is women?
(3)

242. What is Scotty's full name and rank?
(2)

243. What is Chekov's first name?
(3)

244. Is Kirk married?
(1)

245. In "The Trouble with Tribbles," who does Kirk think started the barroom fight?
(2)

246. What was Khan's profession before he was put in suspended animation? ("Space Seed")
(4)

247. Who has the helmsman's position in "Space Seed"?
(4)

248. Who invented Scotch?
(10)

249. Who mapped Sherman's Planet? ("The Trouble with Tribbles")
(4)

250. In which episode do you find someone smoking on the *Enterprise?*
(4)

251. In "The Trouble with Tribbles," who orders the Priority-1 distress call?
(3)

252.

"No, but if you hum a few bars I can fake it." Name any three episodes in which Spock plays his Vulcan harp. (5)

chapter five

EAT, DRINK,
AND BE MERRY

253. In "Charlie X," Yeoman Rand is playing a solitaire card game of sorts when Charlie comes over and performs astounding magical card effects. Now, strain your brain, and describe the pattern on the backs of those cards.
(5)

254. What is the drink McCoy offers Kirk in "The Ultimate Computer"?
(5)

255. In "And the Children Shall Lead," what is Steve's favorite ice-cream mixture?
(5)

256. If Scotty were to come into your space bar this moment and ask for "the usual," what would you give him?
(4)

257. What does the trader from "The Trouble with Tribbles" use to polish his Spican flame gems? (2)

258. In "The Squire of Gothos," what color is the wine? (5)

259. In "Mudd's Women," what game does Eve play instead of solitaire? (4)

260. According to the episode "Miri," what are "mommies"? (5)

261. What is a "foolie"? ("Miri") (3)

262. What is the drink Balok offers Kirk, McCoy, and Bailey in "The Corbomite Maneuver"? (2)

263. Why does McCoy change Kirk's diet card in "The Corbomite Maneuver"? (4)

264. What two Earth games are mentioned in "The Corbomite Maneuver"? (5)

265. What play do the Karidian Players perform for the crew of the *Enterprise* in "The Conscience of the King"? (2)

266. Which song does Uhura sing to Riley in "The Conscience of the King"?
(4)

267. What material poisons Riley in "The Conscience of the King"?
(4)

268. When the *Enterprise* accidentally acquires another guest in "Tomorrow Is Yesterday," what does that guest half-jokingly request for food?
(1)

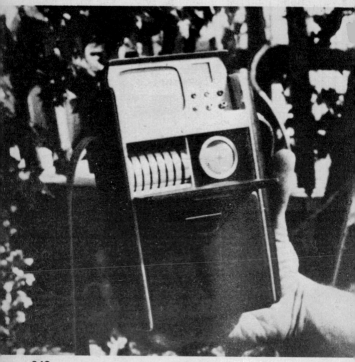

269.

This is:
   a. a communicator
   b. a futuristic slot machine
   c. a tricorder
   d. a phynberg oscillating framizam

(1)

chapter six

TREKNOLOGY

270. What are the coordinates of the council chamber on Gideon? ("The Mark of Gideon")
(4)

271. Which is noisier, the Klingon or the Federation transporter?
(2)

272. What is kironide? ("Plato's Stepchildren")
(3)

273. According to "Spock's Brain," what does the number 7 represent on the industrial scale?
(5)

274. In "Assignment: Earth," how does the *Enterprise* get back to the twentieth century?
(3)

275. What is a subcutaneous transponder?
(3)

276. In "Return to Tomorrow," what does Kirk say the energy-beings will offer Scott?
(5)

277. According to "A Private Little War," how many centuries were there between the development of the iron forge and the flintlock on Earth?
(4)

278. What piece of machinery is the basis for all the *Enterprise*'s major equipment? ("A Piece of the Action")
(5)

279. How much harder is tritanium than steel? ("Obsession")
(4)

280. According to "Friday's Child," what is the Capellan's basic weapon?
(3)

281. In "That Which Survives," when the alien woman/android Losira comes aboard the *Enterprise* and asks about a certain piece of machinery, Engineer John Watkins says it is the cutoff switch of the matter/antimatter integrator control. What is it, really?
(4)

282. What is used to light the cave in "Friday's Child"?
(4)

283.

This is Ensign Chekov, who did not get even a single gray hair while the rest of the landing party was aging in "The Deadly Years." Why?
(3)

284. Why doesn't anything from the *Enterprise* work on Zefrem Cochrane's planetoid? ("Metamorphosis")
(3)

285. In "Catspaw," what is the alien's basic tool?
(5)

286. How does Captain Kirk of the Mirror Universe wipe out his enemies? ("Mirror, Mirror")
(2)

287.

Which episode?
(5)

288. One of Nomad's energy bolts is equal to how many photon torpedos? ("The Changeling")
(4)

289. How fast are Nomad's energy bolts? ("The Changeling")
(3)

290. In "Who Mourns for Adonis?", what kind of energy does Spock suggest might punch a hole in the force field?
(4)

291. In "The City on the Edge of Forever," to what does Spock compare the equipment he is working with?
(2)

292. How many dilithium crystals do *both* Lazaruses steal in "The Alternative Factor"?
(2)

293. In "Errand of Mercy," how do Kirk and Spock destroy the Klingon munition dump?
(3)

294. In "The Devil in the Dark," what kind of phasers do the miners have?
(4)

295. In "A Taste of Armageddon," how is the *Enterprise* presumed destroyed?
(3)

296. In "A Taste of Armageddon," what sort of offensive weapons (besides computers) does Eminiar VII have?
(3)

297. What does Kirk's attorney, in "Court-Martial," prefer to computers?
(1)

298. What is the substitute fuel in "The *Galileo Seven*" that Scotty uses to charge up the *Galileo?*
(3)

299. In "Balance of Terror," what are the Romulans' main weapons?
(2)

300. What kind of gun does Sulu find in "Shore Leave"?
(3)

301. In "The Menagerie," what does it mean when Captain Pike's wheelchair emits two flashes?
(1)

302. In "The Menagerie I," what has Spock programmed the computers to do if the directional controls are tampered with?
(4)

303. In "The Man Trap," what is the setting on Kirk's phaser when he shoots Professor Crater?
(2)

304. In "All Our Yesterdays," who controls the atavachron?
(3)

305. How do you use an agonizer?
(2)

306. How long is the *Enterprise?* (in feet or meters)
(10)

307. Who invented quadrotriticale?
(3)

308. What is the Klingon hand weapon called?
(2)

309. Which finger presses down the trigger on a Klingon hand weapon?
(5)

310. What kind of typewriter does Gary Seven own? ("Assignment: Earth")
(10)

311. What do the Troyians call dilithium crystals? ("Elaan of Troyius")
(5)

312. Define "red-zone proximity."
(4)

313. According to "The Doomsday Machine," what is the densest *alloy* in the galaxy?
(5)

314. In which episode does the *Enterprise* crew have lasers instead of phasers?
    (1)

315. In what century does "Star Trek" take place?
    (2)

316. What is another name for the Chamber of Ages? ("The Devil in the Dark")
    (3)

317. What shields the crew from Delta rays on Class-J starships?
    (4)

318. Which make of pistol does Wyatt Earp prefer? ("Spectre of the Gun")
    (5)

319. In which episode is it stated that no natural phenomenon can move faster than light?
    (3)

320. What is the temperature of a pistol phaser's beam set on "dematerialize"?
    (10)

321. How much does McCoy have to increase the dosage of the tranquilizer to knock out Van Gelder in "Dagger of the Mind"?
    (3)

322. What kills Compton in "Wink of an Eye"?
    (4)

323.

Although the transporter is used in almost every "Star Trek" episode, the *true* Trek fanatic should be able to name the episode this photo is from.
(10)

324. What is the disease in "The Mark of Gideon" that Kirk carries and that almost kills a woman named Odona?
    (10)

325. What kind of medicine does Dr. M'Benga specialize in? ("A Private Little War")
    (4)

326. Where is the cure for "xenopolycythemia" found?
    (3)

327. What is formazine?
    (4)

328. What is the amount of cordrazine used to bring an unconscious person to consciousness?
    (2)

329. What is the "Bubonic Plague of the twenty-third century"?
    (5)

330. In "The Cloud-Minders," what is the material that will stop the plant bacteria on Alpha II from spreading?
    (2)

331. What is the only known antidote for Rigellian fever?
    (5)

332. What is the "Rigellian kassaba fever"? (not related to Rigellian fever)
    (3)

333. In "Wink of an Eye," where is the substance that "accelerates" the body?
(2)

334. In "The Tholian Web," what counteracts the effects of interspace?
(4)

335. In which *two* episodes is a "tri-ox" compound used?
(3)

336. In "For the World Is Hollow and I Have Touched the Sky," what disease is McCoy dying from?
(4)

337. What is stokaline? ("By Any Other Name")
(5)

338. In "The Apple," what drug counteracts the effect of the spore-shooting plants?
(5)

339.

Kirk is about to say:
   a. "What the hell happened?!"
   b. *"Somebody* close that door."
   c. "It's dead."
   d. "So this is what Red Dye #2 does to mice."
(2)

chapter seven

HAIRY
SITUATIONS

340. In "The Tholian Web," how long is it between the first and second interphase?
(5)

341. How many times has Kirk been presumed dead? (Name *at least two* of the episodes.)
(4)

342. Who is the last person to fall prey to Lenore Karidian's killing frenzy? ("The Conscience of the King")
(2)

343. How many times does McCoy have to fire his phaser in order to kill the salt monster in "The Man Trap"?
(2)

344. How long does it take before human tissue starts to disintegrate under constant exposure to Berthold rays? ("This Side of Paradise")
(2)

345. According to "Space Seed," what was the last era of world wars called?
(2)

346. What causes the *Enterprise* to return to the twentieth century in "Tomorrow Is Yesterday"?
(3)

347. In "The Man Trap," what kind of plant supposedly poisons Darnell?
(4)

348. In "Tomorrow Is Yesterday," remember when Captain Christopher's plane was torn apart by the tractor beam? *Why* did it collapse?
(2)

349. Where did Joe Tormolen stab himself? ("The Naked Time")
(1)

350. According to Scott, in "The Naked Time," how long does it take to start the engines of the *Enterprise* after they have been shut off?
(3)

351. During "The Enemy Within," where does Kirk first meet his double?
(3)

352.

Engineer Montgomery Scott is here astonished to find that something extraordinary has happened to the ship's armory. All of the weapons have been mysteriously transformed into primitive fighting instruments, such as sabers, swords, and axes. One in particular attracts the attention of the Scotsman. What is it called?
(4)

353. What eventually smashes into Harry Mudd's ship and destroys it in "Mudd's Women"?
(3)

354. In "Mudd's Women," why does the *Enterprise* have to get to Rigel XII?
(2)

355. In "The Enemy Within," how does Kirk (the good one) tell the crew to identify the evil double?
(3)

356. In "Charlie X," what does the meat loaf turn into?
(2)

357. What is the main poison in a borgia plant?
(4)

358. Which member of the *Enterprise* crew do the Onlies capture in "Miri"?
(1)

359. What kills Dr. Adams in "Dagger of the Mind"?
(3)

360. What does Kirk refer to as "flypaper" in "The Corbomite Maneuver"?
(5)

361. How was Captain Pike exposed to the Alpha rays that caused him to get those ripples on his body and leave him paralyzed? ("The Menagerie I")
(10)

362. In "The Conscience of the King," how is Kirk almost killed?
(3)

363. How is Kirk sentenced to be executed in "The Squire of Gothos"?
(2)

364. Why must Captain Christopher be returned to Earth in "Tomorrow Is Yesterday"?
(2)

365. According to "Court-Martial," what alert (red alert, yellow alert, lavender alert, etc.) was the *Enterprise* on when Kirk jettisoned the pod containing Officer Finney?
(4)

366. How does Kirk explain Spock's ears to a police officer in the 1930s in "The City on the Edge of Forever"?
(3)

367. What is the drug McCoy injects into Sulu in "The City on the Edge of Forever," and which he then pumps into himself by mistake?
(1)

368. What kills Dr. Lester's research group on Camus II? ("Turnabout Intruder")
(4)

369. What was Kirk's crime in Sarpeidon's past? ("All Our Yesterdays")
(4)

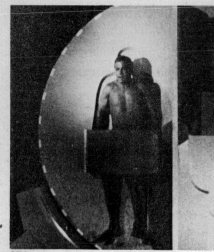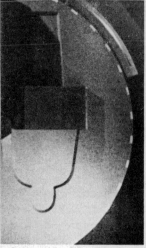

370.

What is happening to Kirk in this picture? He is:
  a. being duplicated
  b. taking a twenty-third-century shower
  c. being disinfected
  d. all of the above
(2)

371. In the beginning of "The City on the Edge of For-
     ever," what causes the *Enterprise*'s rough ride?
     (4)

372. In "Amok Time," what does McCoy slip in with
     the tri-ox compound that simulates death?
     (2)

373. What "part" of Apollo does the *Enterprise* first
     encounter in "Who Mourns for Adonis?"?
     (1)

374. In "The Changeling," what does Nomad do to Uhura?
(2)

375. How does the Companion attack Spock in "Metamorphosis"?
(3)

376. What disease is affecting Miss Hedford in "Metamorphosis"?
(5)

377. What caused the inhabitants of Talos IV to move underground? ("The Menagerie")
(3)

378. In "Journey to Babel," who attacks Kirk with a knife?
(4)

379. In "The Deadly Years," what causes the aging?
(1)

380. Who is the first member of the *Enterprise* crew to show marked signs of aging in "The Deadly Years"?
(3)

381. In "The Gamesters of Triskelion," how do Kirk, Uhura, and Chekov get to Triskelion?
(2)

382. What emotion do the Vulcans of the *Intrepid* feel when they are eaten up by the giant amoeba in "The Immunity Syndrome"?
(4)

383.

In this picture, Spock is discovering that:
  a. Hortas radiate a temperature of 2374° F.
  b. Hortas make him sneeze
  c. the Horta is a wounded animal in great pain
  d. when he gets close to a Horta he has to close his eyes
     because he can't bear the ugliness
(2)

384. In "The Immunity Syndrome," how does Scotty slow the ship when it is being drawn toward the amoeba?
(5)

385. What is the plant that Nona, the "witch woman," uses to cure Kirk in "A Private Little War"?
(2)

386. In "Patterns of Force," what is Spock's "Nazi" rank?
(5)

387. What is the mission of the *Enterprise* in "Patterns of Force"?
(4)

388. In "The Omega Glory," what food is Kirk offered by Captain Tracy?
(10)

389. In "The Omega Glory," which specific substance, when taken out of the human body, leaves behind little white crystals?
(3)

390. Who "gets in the way" when the M-5 needs more power in "The Ultimate Computer"?
(4)

391. According to Spock in "Bread and Circuses," how many people died in Earth's Third World War?
(5)

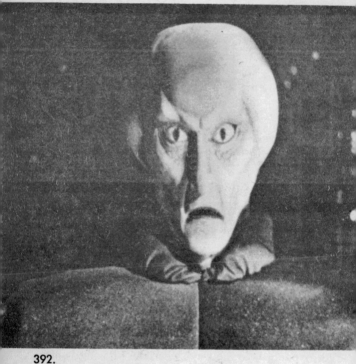

392.

What is this thing called?
a. Balok
b. Maalox
c. Tan Ru
d. Irving

(2)

chapter eight

ALIENS
(HUMANOID)

393. In which episode is a Klingon shown *without* a beard? What are his name and his mission?
     (3)

394. How does Landru communicate with the people that are "of the body" in "The Return of the Archons"?
     (3)

395. What three Organians impose the treaty of peace between the United Federation and the Klingon Empire?
     (5)

396. In "Patterns of Force," what is the name of Isak's older brother?
     (5)

397. What is the name of the leader of the Onlies in "Miri"?
(2)

398. Which is the first episode in which we see the Romulans?
(2)

399. In what episode do the Metrons appear?
(2)

400. When Kirk and Spock beam down to the planet in "Errand of Mercy," who is it that greets them?
(4)

401. In "The Alternative Factor," when Lazarus is first found, what is his body temperature?
(10)

402. In "Amok Time," who is the "other man" in T'Pring's life?
(2)

403. Who is the only person ever to turn down a seat in the Federation Council? ("Amok Time")
(2)

404. According to Apollo in "Who Mourns for Adonis?" who or what killed Agamemnon and Hercules?
(4)

405. In "Who Mourns for Adonis?", who is Apollo's twin brother?
(4)

406. In "Mirror, Mirror," who has the dilithium crystals that *both* universes want?
(3)

407. Koloth is Klingon captain in which episode?
(2)

408. Is Landru a person?
(1)

409. In "Journey to Babel," what type of physiology does Spock claim is similar to Vulcan?
(4)

410. What is the formal title for a Capellan leader? ("Friday's Child")
(3)

411. Of what is Akaar the leader in "Friday's Child"?
(3)

412. What is the Capellan salute? ("Friday's Child")
(5)

413. What is the "Argelian empathic contact"? ("Wolf in the Fold")
(4)

414. Who is Kirk's drill thrall in "The Gamesters of Triskelion"?
(3)

415. In "Let That Be Your Last Battlefield," where the aliens are half black and half white, on which side is Bele white?
(5)

416. In "A Private Little War," what's so special about Nona?
(4)

417. In "A Private Little War," who gave the villagers weapons?
(3)

418. In "The Omega Glory," what are the full names for "Yangs" and "Kohms"?
(2)

419. In "Assignment: Earth," what happened to agents 201 and 347?
(5)

420. What is "Gary Seven" the code name for? ("Assignment: Earth")
(4)

421. In "The Trouble with Tribbles," how does Kirk find out that Darvin is a Klingon spy?
(2)

422. In the episode "Spock's Brain," who are the "Others"?
(3)

423. Who was the medicine chief before Kirk in "This Side of Paradise"?
(4)

424. Who is the Klingon leader in "Day of the Dove"?
(3)

425. What is Natira high priestess of?
(3)

426. What is another word for "Platonian"? ("Plato's Stepchildren")
(4)

427. How are the Platonians' powers transmitted? ("Plato's Stepchildren")
(4)

428. In "Plato's Stepchildren," who is Parmen's wife?
(5)

429. Who is the "queen" of the Scalosians in "Wink of an Eye"?
(2)

430. In "Whom Gods Destroy," what does Marta's dance remind Spock of?
(4)

431. Who is the keeper of Sarpeidon's "library of the past"? (Sarpeidon is the doomed planet of "All Our Yesterdays.")
(3)

432. What is the word for "slave" on Triskelion? ("The Gamesters of Triskelion")
(2)

433. Gary Seven's mission on Earth is to help Terrans to mature into peaceful people. What is his street address?
(10)

434. Who is the sheriff of Tombstone in "Spectre of the Gun"?
(3)

435. "Kahless, the ———" (Kahless is the nasty that set the pattern for all Klingons to follow.) ("The Savage Curtain")
(2)

436. What is the form of address for a Dohlman of Elas? ("Elaan of Troyius")
(3)

437. Without looking at any photos, over which shoulder is Apollo's gown fastened? ("Who Mourns for Adonis?")
(5)

438. When was Flint born? ("Requiem for Methuselah")
    (10)

439. Who/what is Akuta? ("The Apple")
    (2)

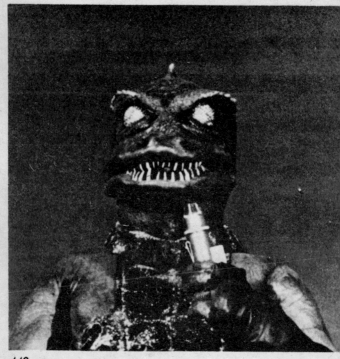

440.

What is the Gorns' reason for destroying the base on Cestus III in "Arena"?
(3)

chapter nine

ALIENS
(NONHUMANOID)

441. In "Return to Tomorrow," who is the first energy-being to introduce himself to the *Enterprise?*
(3)

442. What is the name of Gary Seven's cat in "Assignment: Earth"?
(3)

443. In "Is There in Truth No Beauty?", why is Ambassador Kollos in the box?
(4)

444. In "The Man Trap," how many times does the salt monster change form?
(10)

445. What kills Sulu's pet when they try putting it "back together" in "The Enemy Within"?
(3)

446. What do you get if you feed a tribble?
(3)

447. How do tribbles "greet" Klingons?
(1)

448. In "The Man Trap," how many salt monsters existed?
(1)

449. What are the three names used for Jack the Ripper in "Wolf in the Fold"?
(5)

450. In "The Gamesters of Triskelion," what is the money used by the "providers" called?
(2)

451. What piece of machinery does the creature of "The Devil in the Dark" "steal"?
(1)

452. According to Spock, the Guardian of Forever speaks in riddles. Why?
(3)

453. What kills the creatures/globs in "Operation: Annihilate!"?
(4)

454. In "Operation: Annihilate!", what, more than anything else, do those creatures resemble?
(3)

455.
What might have been this creature's last words?

  a. "In my world, I was King."
  b. "I always liked the dry look."
  c. "*Please* pass the salt!"
  d. "Wake me when we reach Antares."

(2)

456.

This is from:
   a. "The Gamesters of Triskelion"
   b. "The Man Trap"
   c. "The Apple"
   d. a Listerine commercial

(3)

457. According to McCoy, what do the tribbles possess that is a great time-saver?
   (2)

458. Is the Companion from "Metamorphosis" male or female?
   (2)

459. What is a sehlat?
    (3)

460. What is the natural state of the cloud-being from
    "Obsession"?
    (5)

461. How do the tribbles get into the storage com-
    partments, food processors, etc., on the space
    station in "The Trouble with Tribbles"?
    (1)

462. Name the only creature in all the history of "Star
    Trek" with poison fangs.
    (2)

463. What is Ambassador Kollos (human, Vulcan,
    Californian, etc.)?
    (3)

464. In "Spectre of the Gun," what language do the
    Melkotians speak?
    (4)

465. How fast is the creature in "The Lights of Zetar"?
    (5)

466. In "The Savage Curtain," what does Yarnek offer
    the evil people if they win?
    (2)

467. Who/what is "Beauregard"?
    (3)

468.

In "The Tholian Web," what's the name of the commander
of the first Tholian vessel?
(10)

469. "Gav" is:
   a. an engineer on the *Enterprise*
   b. a top NBC executive
   c. a blue-skinned Andorian
   d. a pig-nosed Tellarite
   (2)

470. What creatures of Maynark IV appear to be in-animate rock crystals until attacking?
   (3)

471. What are the names of the only other two things of Sargon's kind? ("Return to Tomorrow")
   (3)

472. What is the Companion from "Metamorphosis" made of?
   (10)

473. In what form does the salt creature beam up to the *Enterprise* in "The Man Trap"? (Whom is the creature impersonating?)
   (3)

474. In which three episodes do we see one or more Andorians?
   (4)

475. About how long is the amoeba of "The Immunity Syndrome"?
   (4)

476. In "Wolf in the Fold," what is the "thing's" food?
   (2)

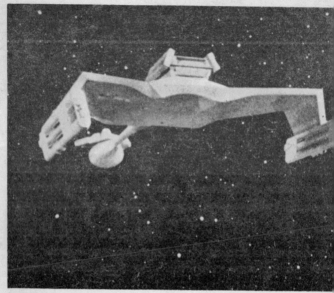

477.

According to Captain Koloth in "The Trouble with Tribbles,"
Klingon ships are not equipped with certain "luxuries."
Which "luxury" is specifically indicated:
   a. cooked meals
   b. soap
   c. liquor
   d. women
(3)

chapter ten

THINGS THAT GO WHOOSH
(SPACESHIPS)

478. On what stardate did Kirk take command of the *Enterprise?*
(10)

479. Only once is it suggested that the *Enterprise* would come apart in "sections"—that the engines could be detached. Which episode?
(5)

480. How many times has the *Enterprise* left its own galaxy?
(3)

481. With what starship is the *Enterprise* scheduled to rendezvous in "Turnabout Intruder"?
(3)

482. In "The Way to Eden," what is the name of the ship that Sevrin pirates?
(3)

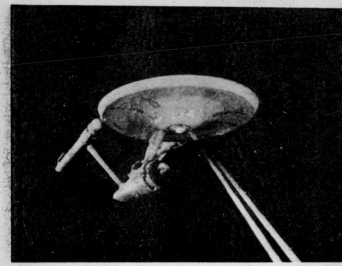

483.

The starship *Enterprise* firing its mighty phasers.
   a. What is its other main form of defensive weaponry?
(1)
   b. On only one episode are the ship's phasers set on
   stun. Which episode, and why?
(5)

484. What is the highest speed that the *Enterprise* has
ever traveled?
   (3)

485. When do we see Uhura's living quarters?
   (5)

486. The Defiant appears (actually, *dis*appears) in
which episode?
   (2)

487. What is the first episode in which the Romulans use Klingon ships?
(3)

488. What is the method of propulsion for the alien ship in "Spock's Brain"?
(2)

489. What is the name of the rocket base in "Assignment: Earth"?
(4)

490. In which episode does the survey vessel S.S. *Beagle* appear?
(4)

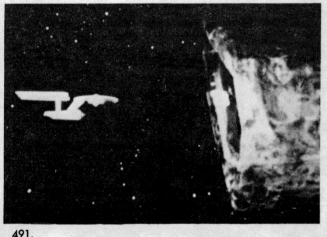

491.
The ship about to be devoured by the Doomsday Machine is not the *Enterprise*. Who is commanding this ship?
(5)

492. In "Bread and Circuses," how does Kirk describe the *Enterprise?*
(3)

493. Which two starships initiate the unscheduled M-5 drills in "The Ultimate Computer"?
(5)

494. On which deck of the *Enterprise* is the Auxiliary Control Center?
(4)

495. Name the starship manned by the Vulcans.
(1)

496. What fuels the main engines of the *Enterprise?*
(1)

497. The *Enterprise* is shown orbiting a planet from right to left only once. In which episode?
(3)

498. In warp speed, how fast can a Star Fleet freighter go?
(4)

499. What powers Khan's spaceship in "Space Seed"?
(3)

500. In which episode do we learn that tnere is a bowling alley on the *Enterprise?*
(4)

501. What is the name and type of spaceship Khan is found on?
(10)

502. In which episode do we see McCoy's living quarters?
(4)

503. In which two episodes do we see airplanes?
(5)

504. How many people on the *Antares*? ("Charlie X")
(4)

505. Near the beginning of "Charlie X," with what does Captain Ramart of the *Antares* compare the *Enterprise*?
(3)

506. In "The Naked Time," what is the mission of the *Enterprise*?
(3)

507. Where on board the *Enterprise* are Yeoman Rand's quarters? ("The Enemy Within")
(10)

508. How many people on Mudd's ship? ("Mudd's Women")
(4)

509. In "Dagger of the Mind," where is Van Gelder first spotted? (deck and section)
(5)

510. In "The Corbomite Maneuver," what is the first space vehicle the *Enterprise* encounters?
(1)

511. What powers the shuttlecraft that contains Kirk and Mendez in "The Menagerie I"?
(3)

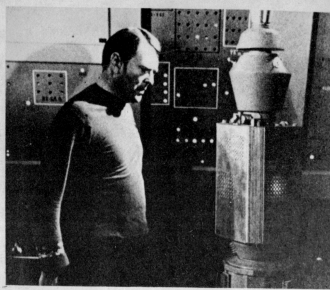

512.

This is a picture of Scotty and Nomad, the superrobot.
  a. What room are they in?
(3)
  b. Why was Nomad originally created? ("The Change-
     ling")
(3)

513. What is the only ship ever to visit Talos IV?
     ("The Menagerie I")
     (2)

514. How many seats in a shuttlecraft?
     (2)

515. The Columbus is:
        a. a starship
        b. a circuit panel on the bridge

    c. a shuttlecraft
    d. Kirk's hairstyle
  (2)

516. How long (in feet) is the shuttlecraft *Galileo*?
("The *Galileo Seven*")
(10)

517. How many ships like the *Enterprise* are there in
the Federation? ("Tomorrow Is Yesterday")
(3)

518. In "Tomorrow Is Yesterday," what is the code
name for Captain Christopher's plane?
(5)

519. According to "Court-Martial," Ben Finney once
left the atomic matter pile circuit open when it
should have been closed. On which ship was this?
(10)

520. In which two episodes is the U.S.S. *Intrepid* mentioned?
(4)

521. Which was the first ship to contact Eminiar VII?
("A Taste of Armageddon")
(5)

522. According to "The Return of the Archons," how
long ago did the U.S.S. *Archon* disappear?
(10)

523. How many times does the *Enterprise* change
course in "Amok Time"?
(10)

524. Once life-support is out on the *Enterprise,* how much longer will the heat and air last? ("The Changeling")
(4)

525. If a starship impulse engine is overloaded, what will be the force in megatons of the explosion? ("The Doomsday Machine")
(10)

526. What is the other *Enterprise*-class ship in "The Doomsday Machine"?
(10)

527. What is the name of the shuttlecraft in "Metamorphosis"?
(2)

528. From what two ships does the *Enterprise* receive phony distress calls in "Friday's Child"?
(4)

529. What is the name of the freighter the M-5 destroys in "The Ultimate Computer"?
(3)

530. What is the other starship-class spaceship besides the *Enterprise* in "The Omega Glory"?
(3)

531. In "Obsession," with which ship was the *Enterprise* scheduled to rendezvous to transfer some medicine?
(3)

532.

Is the shuttlecraft entering or leaving the hangar bay in this picture?
(1)

533. According to "Obsession," on what starship did Kirk serve as an ensign?
(4)

534. What is the mission of the *Enterprise* in "The Deadly Years"?
(4)

535. On board the good ship *Enterprise,* where are the captain's quarters?
(4)

536.

"The Other," the one that merged with Nomad to form a super robot-computer, was called:
   a. Tan Ru
   b. Klarset
   c. Klee-fah
   d. Oy-vey
(2)

chapter eleven

ELECTRONIC FRIENDS
AND ENEMIES
(ROBOTS, ANDROIDS, COMPUTERS)

537. The *Enterprise* has been totally taken over by electronic brains in only two episodes. Which ones?
(3)

538. In "The Changeling," how does Nomad describe women?
(4)

539. When was the *original* Nomad launched? ("The Changeling")
(4)

540. In all 79 "Star Trek" episodes, there were two entirely different "M-5" computers. Give the names of the creators of both.
(2 for one name; 5 for both)

541. In which room is the computer commonly known as Landru?
(3)

542. What is the "abort destruct" order on the *Enterprise?* ("Let That Be Your Last Battlefield")
(10)

543. Which "Star Trek" character owns a type Beta-5 computer?
(5)

544. In "The Ultimate Computer," why does the M-5 recommend that Captain Kirk and McCoy *not* beam down to the planet?
(4)

545. In "The Ultimate Computer," what does "M-5" stand for?
(2)

546. How does Spock, in "The Ultimate Computer," describe the M-5?
(3)

547. In "Return to Tomorrow," what is the device that makes an android's arm move?
(5)

548. In "I, Mudd," which android takes control of the *Enterprise?*
(1)

549. What is the word that to androids means nothing, but "seems to mean something to humans"? ("I, Mudd")
(2)

550. Who is Harry Mudd's wife? ("I, Mudd")
(2)

551. In "The Doomsday Machine," what is the planet killer's hull made of?
(3)

552. Guardian of Forever—machine or being?
(1)

553. In which episode do we hear a computer giggle?
(4)

554. How many stripes does Norman, the android, have on his sleeve on board the *Enterprise?*
(3)

555. According to "Dagger of the Mind," did Dr. Noel ever have any training in hyperpower circuits?
(3)

556. According to the android copy of Kirk in "What Are Little Girls Made Of?", do androids eat?
(3)

557. In "What Are Little Girls Made Of?", how many androids do we see on Exo III?
(3)

558. Who were Ruk's builders?
(2)

559. What is the name of Dr. Korby's male assistant in "What Are Little Girls Made Of?"? (not Ruk)
(4)

560. According to Spock in "What Are Little Girls Made Of?", Dr. Korby was often called the
_____.
(4)

561.

What were the most common words to come out of this box
in Star Trek?

    a. "Beam me/us up."
    b. "Captain!"
    c. "Watch it, Rubber Duck, there's a Smokey on your
       tail!"
    d. "Kirk to *Enterprise*."
(2)

chapter twelve

ALL HAILING FREQUENCIES OPEN . . .

562. When is the *Enterprise* called a UFO?
(4)

563. What is the name of the toothpaste we see briefly advertised in a magazine on Planet 893-IV? ("Bread and Circuses")
(5)

564. Who sponsors the Karidian Players' tours? ("The Conscience of the King")
(4)

565. What is Natira's "bible" called? ("For the World Is Hollow and I Have Touched the Sky")
(3)

566. What do the Onlies call communicators in "Miri"?
(4)

567. On what radio frequency is Rigel XII? ("Mudd's Women")
    (10)

568. How long does it take for a subspace message to reach Star Fleet Command from the edge of the Romulan neutral zone? ("The *Enterprise* Incident")
    (5)

569. What is the one black-and-white segment in "Bread and Circuses"?
    (4)

570. In "Bread and Circuses," what does "Condition Green" mean?
    (2)

571. What is the Federation code the Romulans broke according to "The Deadly Years"?
    (3)

572. What is Kirk's mission in "Friday's Child"?
    (4)

573. In "The Changeling," what is the first method Nomad uses to communicate with the *Enterprise?*
    (4)

574. What is a "flop"? ("The City on the Edge of Forever")
    (3)

575. In the beginning of "Errand of Mercy," Uhura receives an "Automatic all-points relay from Star Fleet Command . . . Code 1!" What does that mean?
(4)

576. In "This Side of Paradise," what one part of communications does Uhura *not* short out?
(2)

577. What is Code 710?
(4)

578. What is the *Enterprise*'s original mission in "Let That Be Your Last Battlefield"?
(4)

579. What is General Order 24? ("A Taste of Armageddon")
(2)

580. What is the message Trelane prints out on the screen of the *Enterprise* in "The Squire of Gothos"?
(1)

581. According to the episode "The Squire of Gothos," what is a secondary form of contact from planet to ship?
(3)

582. By what instrument of communication was the Romulan–Federation treaty set?
(5)

583. On board the Romulan ship in "Balance of Terror," why is Decius, a Romulan officer, reduced two steps in rank?
(4)

584. What is General Order 7?
(4)

585. What is the penalty for breaking General Order 4?
(3)

586. How does Balok identify himself in "The Corbomite Maneuver"?
(4)

587. In "Charlie X," what reason does Charlie give for shorting out the *Enterprise*'s subspace radio?
(2)

588. In "The Man Trap," when Kirk finds that an intruder is aboard, what security condition does he call?
(5)

589. According to regulations, how often are research personnel on an alien planet required to have a physical? ("The Man Trap")
(4)

590. What is a Code 1 emergency?
(2)

591. What form of communication does the *Enterprise* use?
(1)

592. How does Kirk introduce himself to aliens in space?
(1)

593. What does Khan's ship use to signal the *Enterprise* —that is, what *type* of communication? ("Space Seed")
(3)

594. In the judicial system of the Federation, what replaces the gavel?
(3)

595.

You will notice that the name of this shuttlecraft is the *Galileo II*. Why number II?
(3)

chapter thirteen

NUMBERS, LETTERS, AND SYMBOLS

596. What is the serial number of the *Enterprise?*
(1)

597. "17.9 years" is the length of time it would take for what task?
(2)

598. What, according to Spock, is the number of tribbles in the space station's storage compartment? ("The Trouble with Tribbles")
(4)

599. What are the three letters preceding *"Enterprise"* on the mirror universe's *Enterprise?* ("Mirror, Mirror")
(1)

600. In "The Doomsday Machine," what gives Spock the right to relieve Commodore Decker of command?
(5)

601. How many stars on the Federation banner?
(5)

602. In what episode is the Federation banner used?
(5)

603. In "Space Seed," how many on Khan's ship survived the suspended animation?
(2)

604. How long was Khan in suspended animation? ("Space Seed")
(2)

605. In "The Immunity Syndrome," how low are the power levels the second time Scott reports the energy drain to Kirk?
(5)

606. For every Klingon at the space station in "The Trouble with Tribbles," how many security officers are there?
(2)

607. How many security officers does Kirk authorize to protect the storage compartment in "The Trouble with Tribbles"?
(2)

608. What is the "Star Trek" monetary unit?
(1)

609. In "The City on the Edge of Forever," what is the company name on the horse-drawn milk truck?
(10)

610. How long do the Klingons have to get out of Federation territory after Kirk discovers they have poisoned the grain in "The Trouble with Tribbles"?
(4)

611. How close does the *Enterprise* come to a Klingon outpost in "The Trouble with Tribbles"?
(3)

612. What time does Janice Rand go off duty in "Charlie X"?
(5)

613. In "The Enemy Within," how cold does it get on Alfa 177 at night?
(4)

614. In "Mudd's Women," how old is Mudd?
(5)

615. Cyrano Jones sells the tribbles to a trader. For what price? ("The Trouble with Tribbles")
(3)

616. How many lithium (later called dilithium) crystals does the *Enterprise* need for her engines?
(4)

617. Who are older, Grups or Onlies? ("Miri")
(1)

618. On Miri's planet, a person ages how much for every hundred years?
(2)

619. In "Dagger of the Mind," what is stenciled on the box that we later find contains the stowaway, Dr. Van Gelder?
(10)

620. According to "The Conscience of the King," how many men did Lenore Karidian murder?
(4)

621. How old is Lenore, Karidian's daughter, in "The Conscience of the King"?
(5)

622. How many people did Kodos kill, and where? ("The Conscience of the King")
(4)

623. What is the significance of "111 Mark 14"?
(5)

624. How many outposts were intended to monitor the neutral zone? ("Balance of Terror")
(10)

625. How old is Finnegan? ("Shore Leave")
(5)

626. In "The *Galileo Seven*," by how much does the crew of the *Galileo* have to lighten the load in order to lift off?
(5)

627. How much in error are Trelane's time computations in "The Squire of Gothos"?
(5)

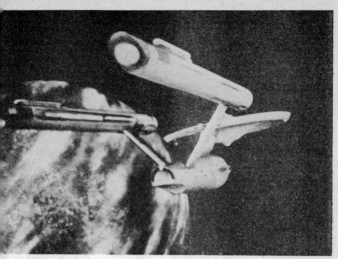

628.

How much did the *Enterprise* cost? ("Mirror, Mirror")
(10)

629. In "Tomorrow Is Yesterday," someone wants to
throw Kirk in jail. For how long?
(2)

630. All right, this is a toughie: What was Captain
Christopher's serial number in "Tomorrow Is Yesterday"?
(10)

631. What time is the Red Hour? ("The Return of
the Archons")
(1)

632. In "A Taste of Armageddon," which two disin-
tegration chambers are destroyed?
(3)

633. What does U.F.P. stand for?
    (1)

634. In "This Side of Paradise," how long has Leila known Spock?
    (3)

635. How many times does the word *"Enterprise"* appear on the starship?
    (3)

636. In "The City on the Edge of Forever," during what time period do Kirk, Spock, and McCoy come to Earth?
    (1)

637. Which of the *Enterprise*'s starcharts shows Earth's system? ("The Changeling")
    (10)

638. How much money did Star Fleet invest in Spock? ("The Apple")
    (10)

639. In "Metamorphosis," what is the constant temperature in Mr. Cochrane's house?
    (3)

640. When was the book *Chicago Mobs of the Twenties* published? ("A Piece of the Action")
    (4)

641. What kind of symbols are on the side of the obelisk from "This Side of Paradise"?
    (3)

642.

"Uhura" means what in Swahili?
   a. love
   b. freedom
   c. beauty
   d. voluptuous
(1)

643. What year does the *Enterprise* return to Earth in
     "Assignment: Earth"?
     (4)

644. What is Scotty's serial number?
     (10)

645.

The words that go with this symbol are:
  a. "May the Force be with you."
  b. "We are One."
  c. "Life is a shadow play."
  d. "Live Long and Prosper."
(3)

chapter fourteen

WHO (OR WHAT) SAID THAT?

646. Fill in the blank: "You are not Morg! You are not ————!"
(2)

647. In "What Are Little Girls Made Of?", what phrase does the real Kirk implant in the mind of the android copy of himself?
(3)

648. Who says this, and in which episode: "That jackass Walsh not only wrecked his own vessel, but in saving his skin we . . ."?
(2)

649. When Sulu is stranded on the planet in "The Enemy Within," how does he suggest the *Enterprise* get some hot coffee to him?
(4)

650. According to Joe Tormolen in "The Naked Time," what are the reasons Sulu should leave him alone? (quote)
(4)

651. In "Charlie X," how did Charlie destroy the *Antares?* (exact quote)
(3)

652. ". . . you botched the acetylcholine (ă-set-il-kō-lēn) test!" Who says that to whom, and in which episode?
(3)

653. What is the chant used to call the Gorgan? ("And the Children Shall Lead")
(5)

654. What is the quote from Milton that Kirk and Kahn use in "Space Seed"?
(4)

655. Who calls Kirk "a stack of books with legs"?
(4)

656. What episode is this from: "In a different reality, I could have called you friend"?
(1)

657. In "Friday's Child," what does Scott say to Chekov after receiving the second distress call?
(4)

658. In "The Trouble with Tribbles," what provokes Scott to belt the Klingon in the chops?
(2)

659.

Lieutenant Commander Leonard McCoy, M.D., otherwise known as "Bones." In "The Man Trap," however, he is on the receiving end of which of the following nicknames?
   a. Cuddles
   b. Sunflower
   c. Plum
   d. Ol' Blue-eyes
(4)

660. What is the last line of "The City on the Edge of Forever"?
     (2)

661. What do "Earthers" remind Korax of? ("The Trouble with Tribbles")
     (3)

662. In "Let That Be Your Last Battlefield," who says: "At warp 10 we're going nowhere mighty fast"?
     (2)

663. What do tribbles remind Spock of? (quote)
(5)

664. In the barroom scene of "The Trouble with Tribbles," what does Korax call Kirk?
(5)

665. According to Mendez in "The Menagerie I," what does R.H.I.P. stand for?
(5)

666. What is Finnegan's nickname for Kirk in "Shore Leave"?
(3)

667. "Are you challenging me to a duel?!" Which episode?
(1)

668. In "A Taste of Armageddon," who calls Kirk a barbarian?
(5)

669. In which episode does someone say that Spock has a hyperactive thyroid?
(3)

670. In which episode does Kirk compare something to a one-color jigsaw puzzle?
(4)

671. In "The Devil in the Dark," what words does the Horta burn into the cavern floor?
(2)

672. "I am not programmed to respond in that area."
What creatures say that, and when?
(1)

673. "Hundreds . . . all human like me. That's ————.
Is that the right word?" Charlie said that in
"Charlie X." Fill in the blank.
(2)

674. In "Errand of Mercy," Kirk's "Go climb a tree"
is the response to what?
(5)

675. In "Errand of Mercy," Kirk is disguised as an
Organian. How does Kor, the Klingon commander, describe him?
(5)

676. Which episode is this from: "You were about to
make a medical comment?"
(3)

677. Which one of "Finagle's Laws" is quoted in
"Amok Time"?
(10)

678. In "Amok Time," what does Spock threaten to
do to McCoy if McCoy doesn't stop "prying" into
his personal affairs?
(4)

679. In "The Trouble with Tribbles," how does Scotty
get rid of all the tribbles on the *Enterprise?* (exact
quote)
(2)

680. Name the episode this is from: "Only a fool fights in a burning house!"
(4)

681. How does Spock explain logic to Norman, the android, in "I, Mudd"?
(5)

682. What frightens Norman away from McCoy, according to Spock, in "I, Mudd"?
(5)

683. According to Spock, what is the tribbles' one redeeming feature?
(3)

684. McCoy: "He talks a lot but he doesn't say much." Who is McCoy referring to?
(3)

685. Who says this: "Well, whaddya know? I finally got the last word."
(1)

686. " 'Payment' is usually expensive." What is Sarek referring to when he says that?
(4)

687. "Fool me once, shame on you. Fool me twice, shame on me." According to "Star Trek," where did this saying originate?
(4)

688.

What is McCoy saying here?
    a. "Live Long and Prosper."
    b. "It's simple if you break your third finger."
    c. "That hurts worse than the uniform."
    d. "But can you crack your knuckles?"
(2)

689. According to Bela Oxmyx in "A Piece of the Action," what kind of man is the most cooperative man in the world?
    (3)

690. What ""superstition" does Spock refer to in "The Immunity Syndrome"?
    (4)

691. In "The Ultimate Computer," what is a "Dunsel"?
    (2)

692. Who says: "We can wallow like a garbage scow against a warp-driven starship"? In which episode?
(3)

693. Whom does Scotty refer to as "loony as an Arcturian dogbird," and in which episode?
(5)

694. What is the correct response to "Queen to Queen's Level Three"?
(5)

695. Which episode is this from?—"I don't like that. I don't believe I ever did. Now I'm sure."
(4)

696. What is the native language of the Klingons?
(2)

697. In "Bread and Circuses," which company sponsors the "Name the Winner" TV show?
(5)

698. Would there ever be a reason to call that pretty young lady, Yeoman Lawton, a lizard?
(5)

699. In "Amok Time," who says: "Art thee Vulcan or art thee human?"
(1)

700. Who gives the name "Gem" to the empath in "The Empath"?
(2)

701. What is Nomad's reason for wiping out the Malurian system in "The Changeling"?
(3)

702. Where and when does Riley plan a "formal dance" in "The Naked Time"?
(3)

703. In "Arena," the universal translator serves what other purpose in addition to translating?
(1)

ANSWERS

Here are the scores for the first chapter. What you should do is add up the gradients for each question answered correctly and compare your number to the table at the end of this section. A score of 115, for example, would mark you as a "Human." Also keep track of your total gradients acquired throughout the book so you can score yourself at the end. (The chart for the entire book's totals is right after the last chapter's table.)

Good luck.

Chapter One
SPACE STATIONS, STARS, GALAXIES, AND ENTIRE CIVILIZATIONS

1. b. Rigel VII. ("The Menagerie")

2. Omicron Ceti III. ("This Side of Paradise")

3. Quadrant 904.

4. The villagers and the hill-people.

5. "Tal-shaya," a swift, almost painless breaking of the neck.

6. Quadrotriticale (some kind of far-out grain).

7. Number 7.

8. "Only a few thousand years old," according to Spock.

9. Star System 892.

10. Bang Bang.

11. 200 years ago.

12. K-type (adaptable for humans with pressure domes).

13. More than four billion.

14. "Errand of Mercy."

15. Landru, in "The Return of the Archons," is the supercomputer god thing that guides almost every person on the planet by means of telepathy.

16. Deep Space Station K-7.

17. Janus VI. ("The Devil in the Dark")

18. Starbase 11.

19. New Paris.

20. Bootes III.

21. Ophiuchus VI.

22. Antares Pi IV.

23. On Colony Alpha 5.

24. It has the cloud city, Stratos. ("The Cloud-Minders")

25. "The Cloud-Minders"; Ardana.

26. Altair VI.

27. Starbase 6.

28. "Tomorrow Is Yesterday," as the builder of the *Enterprise*.

29. "About Stage D-minus."

30. Pergium.

31. Tantalus V.

32. It isn't. Kirk only made it up. (He *says* that it's played on Beta Antares IV, however.)

33. Ganymede.

34. "Court-Martial."

35. The Minarian star system's.

36. Asteroids should have smashed it to bits by now. (It's in an asteroid belt.)

37. Sol.

38. The Gamma 7A system.

39. "The beginnings of industrialization."

40. Planet M-113.

41. Planet 892-IV. ("Bread and Circuses")

42. Planet Exo III.

43. Elas. ("Elaan of Troyius")

44. Marcos XII.

45. Kelva.

46. Zeon and Ekos. ("Patterns of Force")

47. Three.

48. Death. (By phaser, by hanging, by electrocution, etc. But according to Harry Mudd, "the key word is d-d-death.")

49. Deneva.

50. A planet called Vendikar.

51. No. ("The Man Trap")

52. Dana Iotia II.

53. On Camus II. ("Turnabout Intruder")

54. Triacus (Trī-á-cus). ("And the Children Shall Lead")

55. Approximately 3,724,000,000.

56. Sandara. (We never heard what their *planet* was called, however.)

57. The Rigel system.

58. Troyius. ("Elaan of Troyius")

59. 1,000.

60. Five (all but two in a seven-planet system).

61. The twenty-third level.

62. Its name and location are kept secret. Gary Seven says the inhabitants of this planet are advanced enough to hide it. (They do hide it; otherwise, the Feds would have found it by now.)

CHAPTER 1
++
    ORGANIAN   187 - 250
++
    VULCAN   162 - 186
++
    TALOSIAN   137 - 161
++
    HUMAN   112 - 136
++
    ANDORIAN   87 - 111
++
    ROMULAN   62 - 86
++
    KLINGON   37 - 61
++
    TRIBBLE   12 - 36
++
    SLIME DEVIL   0 - 11
++

Chapter Two
DECISIONS, DECISIONS . . .

63. "The Naked Time."

64. Tharn is afraid they will be used for war.

65. "That Which Survives."

66. "Instrument failure caused a navigational error." (Fat chance!)

67. He failed a psychosimulator test.

68. In "The Apple," because Scott can't counteract the energy drain affecting the ship.

69. It is titled "Survey on Cyginian Respiratory Diseases."

70. Whether or not to admit the Coridan System into the Federation.

71. With precious stones. (Kirk then says that these could be easily reproduced on the *Enterprise*.)

72. He felt responsible for the lives of his crew. (They were destroyed by the planet killer.)

73. James Kirk.

74. Whether or not to destroy about one million peo-

ple on Deneva so that others would live. ("Operation: Annihilate!")

75. He "approves" of hobbies (such as electronics).

76. They make all fighting instruments red-hot.

77. Kirk, who is then followed by Kang's "This is Kang. Cease hostilities." (Those Klingons never did have much of a way with words.)

78. Sulu.

79. Yes.

80. Electrifying the outside of the ship.

81. "Probably somebody's discovered a hangnail."

82. His adrenaline.

83. "Blast it," or, in other words, fire at it with phasers.

84. He wants asylum (from the penal colony on the planet).

85. "You're hungry."

86. To act as a flare, which the retreating *Enterprise* might see.

87. In a closet.

88. A career in bioresearch.

89. Galaxy travel without flight plan, effecting a menace to navigation, and operating a space vessel without master's papers.

90. Number 1.

91. The engineering deck.

92. No, not "medium rare." He likes it loose.

93. What he says is, "No more than twelve at a time." However, two Klingons are already at the station, so only ten more can beam over.

94. Spock.

CHAPTER 2

++
| ORGANIAN | 70 - 94 |
++
| VULCAN | 61 - 69 |
++
| TALOSIAN | 51 - 60 |
++
| HUMAN | 42 - 50 |
++
| ANDORIAN | 32 - 41 |
++
| ROMULAN | 23 - 31 |
++
| KLINGON | 14 - 22 |
++
| TRIBBLE | 4 - 13 |
++
| SLIME DEVIL | 0 - 3 |
++

Chapter Three
SPOCKOLOGY

95. He's just seen his paycheck. But seriously . . . Spock has been affected by the virus in "The Naked Time." It brings out the inner emotions in everybody. In Spock, it's "I could never tell my mother I loved her."

96. The Lirpa.

97. Of course. Spock knows everything.

98. *No!* The Romulans are an offshoot of the Vulcans.

99. Because of traces of nickel and copper in his blood.

100. T-negative.

101. Amanda.

102. a. First Officer in an alternate universe (aboard the U.S.S. *Enterprise*). Spock would like it to stay that way, for someone is always trying to knock off the captain. It's from "Mirror, Mirror." (By the way, have you ever wondered what the Klingons are like in the mirror universe?)

103. The library/computer station.

104. There is no such thing. (It is used as a bluff in "The *Enterprise* Incident.")

105. In "Is There in Truth No Beauty?" (The IDIC is a pendant that Spock wears; the initials stand for "Infinite Diversity in Infinite Combinations.")

106. A-7 computer expert.

107. "Where his liver should be," according to McCoy in "A Private Little War."

108. S 179-276 SP. ("Court-Martial")

109. As far as we, the "Star Trek" viewers, have seen, it is several parsecs. This was shown when Spock "felt" the 400+ Vulcans die on board the U.S.S. *Intrepid*. ("The Immunity Syndrome")

110. "The Doomsday Machine," when Spock threatens to relieve Decker of command. Decker says, "You're bluffing!" And we all know Spock's classic answer.

111. Nome (meaning "All things").

112. Pon far.

113. Eighteen years.

114. The day when Flint (alias Da Vinci, Brahms, Solomon, etc.) eventually dies. ("Requiem for Methuselah")

115. 102.437 years old (102 is acceptable).

116. Pan. (Must be those pointy ears.)

117. Salmon, and the giant eel-birds of Regulus V.

118. Seven.

119. "The blood fever." As spoken by T'Pau: "He is in Plak tow, the blood fever."

120. This is from the episode "This Side of Paradise." Spock has been affected by the "spores" (given off by certain plants), which give any human (or Vulcan) a carefree attitude (they also protect you from Berthold rays).

121. "A dealer in kevas and trillium."

122. A dragon.

123. "Dipping little girls' curls in inkwells."

124. "The *Galileo Seven*." (And a good thing, too.)

125. Yes, but only on rare occasions. (Very rare, such as alcohol in medicine. This is because Vulcans are very susceptible to alcohol. A drink or two will knock them right out.)

126. "Dagger of the Mind," to get through the mind block the neural neutralizer has put on Van Gelder.

127. "Pulse 242; blood pressure almost nonexistent."

128. Forty-seven (Earth included).

129. Yes, in "Charlie X."

130. Charlie Evans in "Charlie X."

131. The shape and size of the Vulcan ear makes it easier to catch sound waves in the thin Vulcan atmosphere. (The points also aid in counting to twelve.)

```
                 CHAPTER 3
+++++++++++++++++++++++++++++++++++++++++++
    ORGANIAN                93 - 125
+++++++++++++++++++++++++++++++++++++++++++
    VULCAN                  81 - 92
+++++++++++++++++++++++++++++++++++++++++++
    TALOSIAN                68 - 80
+++++++++++++++++++++++++++++++++++++++++++
    HUMAN                   56 - 67
+++++++++++++++++++++++++++++++++++++++++++
    ANDORIAN                43 - 55
+++++++++++++++++++++++++++++++++++++++++++
    ROMULAN                 31 - 42
+++++++++++++++++++++++++++++++++++++++++++
    KLINGON                 18 - 30
+++++++++++++++++++++++++++++++++++++++++++
    TRIBBLE                  6 - 17
+++++++++++++++++++++++++++++++++++++++++++
    SLIME DEVIL              0 - 5
+++++++++++++++++++++++++++++++++++++++++++
```

Chapter Four
SPACE PEOPLE

132. a. SC 937-0176 CEC. ("Court-Martial")
    b. "Balance of Terror." Kirk must beam aboard a Romulan ship to steal the cloaking device—so he has to make up like a Romulan—or *else.*

133. Seven.

134. Two ("I, Mudd" and "Mudd's Women").

135. Angela Martine and Robert Tomlinson. (Tomlinson is later killed in the Romulan attack.)

136. Tarsus IV.

137. Captain James Kirk. (To Korax, Kirk is more like a Denebian slime devil.)

138. His father, the former medicine chief, died before he was able to pass on the knowledge.

139. The Deputy Führer of Ekos. (He is murdered by a rebel named Isak.)

140. Twenty.

141. Who else? James Kirk. ("Court-Martial")

142. Merikus.

143. Izar. ("Whom Gods Destroy")

144. Lee.

145. Here are all seven:
   1. Palm Leaf of Axanar Peace Mission
   2. Grankite Order of Tactics, Class of Excellence
   3. Prantares Ribbon of Commendation, First and Second Class
   4. Medal of Honor

     5. Silver Palm with Cluster
     6. Star Fleet Citation for Conspicuous Gallantry
     7. Karagite Order of Heroism

146. Captain Kirk. ("The Savage Curtain")

147. A huge scar, running down almost the entire length of his face.

148. Admiral Komak.

149. Marlena Moreau.

150. "Spectre of the Gun."

151. Dr. Joseph Boyce.

152. Seventeen. That is, she *looks* seventeen; she is actually around fifty.

153. John Burke. (Ivan Burkoff is Chekov's misnomer for him.)

154. "Wiving settlers."

155. Lieutenant Mira Romaine. ("The Lights of Zetar")

156. Governor Cory.

157. Chekov has no brother. In "Day of the Dove," however, he has a *fictional* brother, Piotr.

158. Mr. Marvick.

159. Tommy Starnes.

160. Kirok.

161. Roberta Lincoln.

162. William B. Harrison.

163. "The Ultimate Computer."

164. Dr. Richard Daystrom. ("The Ultimate Computer")

165. Ron Tracy.

166. John Gill.

167. "A woman." That's all we hear of that subject.

168. Rigel IV.

169. Ensign David Garrovick.

170. Eight years younger.

171. Commodore Stocker.

172. She is to prevent a war on Epsilon Canaris III.

173. He discovered the space warp.

174. Lieutenant Palmer.

175. Commodore.

176. Kirk, McCoy, Scott, and Uhura.

177. Jackson Roykirk.

178. Lieutenant Carolyn Palamas.

179. Lieutenant Kyle. ("Who Mourns for Adonis?")

180. Pink.

181. Thirty-four.

182. Twenty-two.

183. George Samuel Kirk, the captain's brother. He lives (or lived) on the planet Deneva. (He is killed by the flying parasites in "Operation: Annihilate!")

184. Ruth.

185. The 21st Street Mission.

186. The bum sitting next to Kirk and Spock in the mission.

187. "The Alternative Factor."

188. Elias Sandoval.

189. Botanist Dimont.

190. Anan 872.

191. Samuel T. Cogley. After Kirk, he defends Ben Finney.

192. Records officer.

193. Captain Christopher.

194. Kirk and Sulu.

195. Sulu and Kirk.

196. "The *Galileo Seven.*"

197. Dr. McCoy.

198. Captain Kirk.

199. Finnegan.

200. He masquerades as Karidian, the actor.

201. Jon Daily.

202. Captain Kirk and Kevin Riley.

203. His "quarterly physical check."

204. He wears the green wraparound shirt.

205. Dr. Janet Wallace.

206. Tristan.

207. Dr. Helen Noel.

208. Kirk.

209. Roger.

210. Christine.

211. Kirk.

212. Two.

213. Ben Childress, Herm Gosset, and Benton.

214. Captain Leo Walsh.

215. Smuggling, transport of stolen goods, purchase of space vessel with counterfeit money.

216. Harcourt Fenton Mudd. ("Mudd's Women")

217. Eve McHuron, Magda Kovacs, Ruth Bonaventure.

218. Jim Farrel.

219. Crewman Fisher.

220. Brandy.

221. Fencing.

222. Spock and Joe Tormolen.

223. Tom Nellis.

224. Charles Evans.

225. Yeoman Janice Rand.

226. "Four oh . . . one hundred percent . . . sound of wind and limb."

227. They are engaged.

228. Tina Lawton (yeoman third class).

229. This is sort of a two-part trick question. First part: there is *one* human (Nancy Crater is not a human). Second part: the *Enterprise* doesn't land; it *never has* landed on a planet. (Give yourself credit only if you spotted both parts.)

230. To Sulu, because he missed mess call.

231. Baroner.

232. The Alpha Centauri system.

233. Leonard.

234. Archaeology-and-Anthropology officer.

235. No one *buys* the first tribble. Uhura, however, is *given* a tribble by Cyrano Jones.

236. Commander Lurry.

237. Lieutenant Marla McGivers.

238. Lieutenant Areel Shaw.

239. The tribbles have stuffed up the food processors.

240. Yes. According to "Whom Gods Destroy," he once was one of the most respected.

241. About one-third.

242. Lieutenant Montgomery Scott.

243. Pavel.

244. No. Well, actually, in "The Paradise Syndrome," he *did* marry an Indian woman, Miramanee, but he was suffering from amnesia and a generally weak mind at the time.

245. Chekov.

246. He was an engineer.

247. Lieutenant Spinelli.

248. "A little old lady in Leningrad." ("The Trouble with Tribbles")

249. John Burke.

250. "A Piece of the Action."

251. Nilz Baris.

CHAPTER 4

++
    ORGANIAN   309 - 413
++
    VULCAN   268 - 308
++
    TALOSIAN   227 - 267
++
    HUMAN   185 - 226
++
    ANDORIAN   144 - 184
++
    ROMULAN   103 - 143
++
    KLINGON   61 - 102
++
    TRIBBLE   20 - 60
++
    SLIME DEVIL   0 - 19
++

Chapter Five
EAT, DRINK, AND BE MERRY

252. "Amok Time," "Charlie X," "The Way to Eden," "Elaan of Troyius," "The Paradise Syndrome."

253. Solid blue.

254. A "Finagle's Folly."

255. "Chocolate wobble and pistachio . . . and apricot."

256. In "Spectre of the Gun," it's "half a gallon of Scotch," but that seems a bit unlikely. Give him a shot of Scotch.

257. Antarean glow water.

258. It isn't wine, it's brandy—and, if you got that right, it's red.

259. Double-jack.

260. "Can-opener things."

261. A game. (That's the Onlies' word for it.)

262. Tranya.

263. Kirk is a few pounds overweight.

264. Chess and poker.

265. Hamlet.

266. "Beyond Antares."

267. ". . . tetralubisol, a highly volatile lubricant in use aboard ship."

268. Chicken soup.

```
             CHAPTER 5
+++++++++++++++++++++++++++++++++++++++++
   ORGANIAN              45 - 61
+++++++++++++++++++++++++++++++++++++++++
   VULCAN                39 - 44
+++++++++++++++++++++++++++++++++++++++++
   TALOSIAN              33 - 38
+++++++++++++++++++++++++++++++++++++++++
   HUMAN                 27 - 32
+++++++++++++++++++++++++++++++++++++++++
   ANDORIAN              21 - 26
+++++++++++++++++++++++++++++++++++++++++
   ROMULAN               15 - 20
+++++++++++++++++++++++++++++++++++++++++
   KLINGON                9 - 14
+++++++++++++++++++++++++++++++++++++++++
   TRIBBLE                3 - 8
+++++++++++++++++++++++++++++++++++++++++
   SLIME DEVIL            0 - 2
+++++++++++++++++++++++++++++++++++++++++
```

Chapter Six
TREKNOLOGY

269. c. a tricorder.

270. 875-020-709.

271. The Federation's. The Klingon transporter is silent. ("Day of the Dove")

272. "Kironide is a particularly potent and long-lasting source of power; very rare."

273. Earth's level of development in 2030.

274. By using the "light-speed breakaway factor."

275. A material injected into the skin that can act as a homing device for a transporter beam. ("Patterns of Force")

276. A starship engine the size of a walnut.

277. "On Earth, about twelve centuries."

278. The transtater.

279. 21.4 times harder than the finest magnesium steel.

280. The kligat, sort of a Frisbee with spikes and razor blades on it.

281. The emergency overload bypass valve of the matter/antimatter integrator.

282. A magnesite-nitron tablet. (When struck with sufficient force, it creates a bright flame that lasts for quite a while.)

283. According to McCoy's medical analysis, when Chekov was almost scared to death, his adrenaline flow increased and counteracted the radiation that caused the aging.

284. Some kind of energy-damping field affects all power units so that they just won't operate.

285. The transmuter.

286. With the tantalus field.

287. "The Tholian Web." (The only episode in which spacesuits are used.)

288. Ninety.

289. They move at warp 15.

290. M-rays.

291. "Stone knives and bearskins."

292. Four.

293. They blow it up with a sonic grenade.

294. Phaser #1s.

295. ". . . classified destroyed by a tricobalt-satellite explosion."

296. Sonic disrupters.

297. Books. (Like McCoy, he's a bit old-fashioned and believes more in people than in machines.)

298. The phaser's energy.

299. Energy-plasma bolts.

300. "An old-time Police Special."

301. "No." (One flash means "yes.")

302. Cross-circuit the vessel's life-support system.

303. Stun.

304. Mr. Atoz.

305. Apply it to the left shoulder. It inflicts pain as a form of punishment. ("Mirror, Mirror")

306. 947 feet or 288.646 meters.

307. The Russians.

308. A disrupter.

309. The thumb.

310. An IBM Model C.

311. Radans.

312. A red-zone proximity occurs when all power is lost in the warp engines. When this happens, the matter/antimatter shielding starts to disintegrate, and the ship will blow up in about four hours. The engines (the cylinder parts of the ship) can be jettisoned, but the ship will then have to proceed on impulse (sublight) power. ("The Savage Curtain")

313. Neutronium.

314. "The Menagerie." (This is before Kirk was captain. Phasers have not yet been invented.)

315. The twenty-third.

316. The Vault of Tomorrow.

317. A baffle plate. ("The Menagerie")

318. A Buntline Special.

319. In "The Lights of Zetar."

320. About 8,000°C ("That Which Survives")

321. He has to triple it.

322. Rael scratches him, which for some unexplained reason causes him to age tremendously and die.

323. "A Taste of Armageddon." You should be able to tell by the wall behind the landing party. Even though the wall is used in another episode, you will note that Spock does not have a tricorder. He does in the other show. By the way, can you name that other episode? It's "Wink of an Eye."

324. Vegan choriomeningitis.

325. Vulcan medicine.

326. On Yonada, a huge asteroid/spaceship world. ("For the World Is Hollow and I Have Touched the Sky")

327. A drug McCoy uses in "By Any Other Name" to make Hanar irritable so that he will start an argument with Rojan.

328. 1 cc. ("Obsession")

329. "Rigellian fever." ("Requiem for Methuselah")

330. Zienite.

331. Ryetalyn. ("Requiem for Methuselah")

332. There is no such thing. McCoy makes it up and Spock pretends to have it so that they can escape from the Kelvans in "By Any Other Name."

333. In the Scalosian water.

334. A diluted theragen derivative.

335. "Amok Time" and "The Tholian Web."

336. Xenopolycythemia.

337. A multivitamin compound injected into the bloodstream.

338. Masiform D.

```
              CHAPTER 6
++++++++++++++++++++++++++++++++++++++++++++
   ORGANIAN              204 - 273
++++++++++++++++++++++++++++++++++++++++++++
   VULCAN                177 - 203
++++++++++++++++++++++++++++++++++++++++++++
   TALOSIAN              150 - 176
++++++++++++++++++++++++++++++++++++++++++++
   HUMAN                 122 - 149
++++++++++++++++++++++++++++++++++++++++++++
   ANDORIAN               95 - 121
++++++++++++++++++++++++++++++++++++++++++++
   ROMULAN                68 - 94
++++++++++++++++++++++++++++++++++++++++++++
   KLINGON                40 - 67
++++++++++++++++++++++++++++++++++++++++++++
   TRIBBLE                13 - 39
++++++++++++++++++++++++++++++++++++++++++++
   SLIME DEVIL             0 - 12
++++++++++++++++++++++++++++++++++++++++++++
```

Chapter Seven
HAIRY SITUATIONS

339. b. *"Somebody close that door."* The tribbles have just been dumped on Kirk from above.

340. Two hours, twelve minutes.

341. *Four*—and here they are: "Amok Time," "The *Enterprise* Incident," "Return to Tomorrow," and "The Tholian Web."

342. Her father, Kodos. (He steps in the path of the phaser shot intended for Kirk.)

343. Twice. (The first time he can't bring himself to kill what looks like his long-lost love.)

344. Human tissue will disintegrate in seventy-two hours.

345. The Eugenics Wars.

346. They are almost drawn into a black star; that puts them in a time warp.

347. A borgia plant.

348. It was not structurally strong enough to withstand the force of the beam.

349. In the intestines, while he was in the ship's galley.

350. Thirty minutes.

351. In the engineering room.

352. A traditional Scottish broadsword. More specifically, a claymore.

353. An asteroid.

354. Rigel XII has lithium crystals, and all of the crystals on the *Enterprise* are shot. (They *can* move—very slowly—on impulse power.)

355. The double has scratches on his face.

356. "Turkeys . . . real turkeys."

357. Alkaloid. ("The Man Trap")

358. Yeoman Janice Rand.

359. He dies of loneliness, inflicted by the neural neutralizer.

360. The rotating cube in front of the *Enterprise,* actually a warning buoy.

361. First of all, they are not Alpha rays, but Delta rays. He is subjected to them on an inspection tour of a cadet vessel. One of the baffle plates ruptures, and he dashes in to try to save the other men, "but the repeated exposure to Delta rays . . ."

362. Somebody puts a phaser-on-overload behind the red-alert light; it almost takes out a deck or two.

363. As Trelane says, "You will hang by your neck, Captain . . . until you are dead! Dead! DEAD!"

364. His not-yet-conceived son, Shaun Christopher, is to head the first Earth–Saturn probe. If Captain Christopher is not returned, there will be no Shaun Christopher and history will be changed.

365. Double red alert.

366. ". . . caught his head in a mechanical—uh—rice picker."

367. Cordrazine.

368. A type of radiation called "celebium."

369. He was accused of being a witch.

370. a. being duplicated. It wasn't his idea, though—it's
Dr. Korby's, in "What Are Little Girls Made Of?"

371. They are passing through "ripples in time."

372. A neural paralyzer.

373. His hand.

374. Wipes out her memory.

375. It gives him "a rather quaint, old-fashioned electric shock . . . of respectable voltage."

376. "Sakuro's disease."

377. The surface of their planet was destroyed by a nuclear war.

378. Thelev, an Orion disguised as an Andorian.

379. Low-frequency radiation, residue from a comet.

380. Scotty is the first *really* to show it. However, Kirk noticed some gray in McCoy's hair a little earlier.

381. They sort of "pop in." There is no shimmer, no flash of light, nothing.

382. Astonishment.

383. c. The Horta is a wounded animal in great pain.

384. By applying *forward* thrust.

385. A mako root.

386. Lieutenant.

387. To locate John Gill, a missing cultural observer.

388. "Barbecued long-necked rabbit-antelope."

389. Water.

390. Ensign Harper. (He is trying to shut off power to the M-5, but the M-5 won't let him.)

391. Thirty-seven million.

```
                    CHAPTER 7
++++++++++++++++++++++++++++++++++++++++++++++
   ORGANIAN                    128 - 171
++++++++++++++++++++++++++++++++++++++++++++++
   VULCAN                      111 - 127
++++++++++++++++++++++++++++++++++++++++++++++
   TALOSIAN                     94 - 110
++++++++++++++++++++++++++++++++++++++++++++++
   HUMAN                        76 - 93
++++++++++++++++++++++++++++++++++++++++++++++
   ANDORIAN                     59 - 75
++++++++++++++++++++++++++++++++++++++++++++++
   ROMULAN                      42 - 58
++++++++++++++++++++++++++++++++++++++++++++++
   KLINGON                      25 - 41
++++++++++++++++++++++++++++++++++++++++++++++
   TRIBBLE                       8 - 24
++++++++++++++++++++++++++++++++++++++++++++++
   SLIME DEVIL                   0 - 7
++++++++++++++++++++++++++++++++++++++++++++++
```

Chapter Eight
ALIENS (HUMANOID)

392. a. Balok, the alter ego of the small Fesarian of the same name. ("The Corbomite Maneuver")

393. "The Trouble with Tribbles." He is a Klingon spy named Darvin. His mission: to poison the quadrotriticale in the space station.

394. By telepathy.

395. Ayelborne, Claymare, and Trefayne.

396. Abrom.

397. Jahn.

398. "Balance of Terror."

399. "Arena."

400. Ayelborne.

401. 98.1° F.

402. Stonn.

403. T'Pau, an influential Vulcan.

404. Apollo.

405. Artemis.

406. The Halkans, a race inhabiting a planet full of dilithium crystals.

407. "The Trouble with Tribbles."

408. No, "he" is a computer. ("The Return of the Archons")

409. Rigellian.

410. Teer.

411. The ten tribes of Capella IV.

412. Verbal: "We come with open hearts, and hands." Nonverbal: The right hand is put over the heart in a fist, then extended palm up.

413. Sort of a voodoo method for finding criminals. All persons connected with the crime, plus the person with the capability to initiate the contact, are seated in a circle, and they join hands. The person with the "old gift" then can discover the criminal.

414. Shana.

415. His left.

416. She is a Kanutu woman. Earth equivalent: female witch doctor.

417. The Klingons. (No reason, just nastiness.)

418. "Yankees" and "Communists."

419. They are killed in a car crash.

420. Supervisor 194.

421. Tribbles hiss at him. Tribbles do *not* hiss at non-Klingons.

422. "The givers of pain and delight," also known as Eymorgs.

423. Salish.

424. Kor.

425. The people of Yonada. ("For the World Is Hollow and I Have Touched the Sky")

426. Academician.

427. By brain waves.

428. Philana.

429. Deela.

430. "It's reminiscent of the dances Vulcan children perform in nursery school."

431. Mr. Atoz.

432. Thrall.

433. 811 East 68th Street, Apt. 12B.

434. Wyatt Earp.

435. Unforgettable.

436. Your Glory.

437. His left.

438. In 3834 B.C., as a Mesopotamian.

439. "The Eyes and Ears of Vaal." *(Ecouter:* French for *listen.)* Vaal is the super-duper computer thingie with a "head" like a dragon.

CHAPTER 8

++
```
  ORGANIAN          131 - 175
```
++
```
  VULCAN            113 - 130
```
++
```
  TALOSIAN           96 - 112
```
++
```
  HUMAN              78 - 95
```
++
```
  ANDORIAN           61 - 77
```
++
```
  ROMULAN            43 - 60
```
++
```
  KLINGON            26 - 42
```
++
```
  TRIBBLE             8 - 25
```
++
```
  SLIME DEVIL         0 - 7
```
++

Chapter Nine
ALIENS (NONHUMANOID)

440. The Federation has invaded Gorn territory. (How Gorny!)

441. Sargon.

442. Isis.

443. The sight of him will drive a human insane.

444. Six times.

445. "The shock of reabsorption was too much for it."

446. As McCoy said, "A whole bunch of hungry little tribbles."

447. Whenever a tribble comes near a Klingon, it starts hissing and squeaking. (The tribble, not the Klingon.)

448. Only one.

449. Beratis, Kesla, and Redjac.

450. Quatloos.

451. The main circulating pump for the reactor of the mining colony on Janus V.

452. So our beloved *Enterprise* crew can understand it.

453. A lot of ultraviolet light.

454. Single brain cells.

455. c. *"Please pass the salt!"* This is the last salt monster. It lives (lived) on salt. ("The Man Trap")

456. c. "The Apple." The picture is of Akuta (the man) standing before his "god," Vaal.

457. "They're born pregnant."

458. Female.

459. The Vulcan equivalent of a Teddy bear. However, as Spock says, "On Vulcan the 'Teddy bears' are alive . . . and have *six-inch fangs*." ("Journey to Babel")

460. Di-kironium, a material that was thought to exist only under laboratory conditions.

461. Through the air vents.

462. A mugato in "A Private Little War." Mugatos are white, ape-like creatures that live on the planet Neural.

463. A Medusan. ("Is There in Truth No Beauty?")

464. Any language at all. They communicate by telepathy, so they appear to be speaking in the listener's native language.

465. Its speed varies. It was, however, recorded going warp 2.6.

466. Power. (That's the sort of people they are—Genghis Khan and associates.)

467. "Beauregard" is Sulu's and Yeoman Rand's pet plant in "The Man Trap." Sulu calls it "Gertrude."

468. Loskene.

469. d. a pig-nosed Tellarite. (He really is pig-nosed —see "Journey to Babel.")

470. Sandbats. ("The Empath")

471. Henoch and Thalassa.

472. A cloud of ionized hydrogen.

473. Crewman Green.

474. "The Gamesters of Triskelion," "Journey to Babel," and "Whom Gods Destroy."

475. The amoeba is about 11,000 miles long.

476. Fear.

++

ORGANIAN	95 – 127

++

VULCAN	82 – 94

++

TALOSIAN	69 – 81

++

HUMAN	57 – 68

++

ANDORIAN	44 – 56

++

ROMULAN	31 – 43

++

KLINGON	19 – 30

++

TRIBBLE	6 – 18

++

SLIME DEVIL	0 – 5

++

Chapter Ten
THINGS THAT GO WHOOSH (SPACESHIPS)

477. d. women. Koloth indicates this by outlining a female with his hands near the end of a scene. It takes a pretty sharp eye to catch. (But in "Day of the Dove," the Klingon ship *does* have at least one woman on board, so this question *only* applies to "The Trouble with Tribbles.")

478. Stardate 1356. ("The Deadly Years")

479. "The Apple." (Kirk to Scotty: "Discard the warp drive nacelles if you have to and crack out of there with the main section . . . but *get my ship out of there!*")

480. Three. ("Where No Man Has Gone Before," "Is There in Truth No Beauty?", and "By Any Other Name")

481. The *Potemkin*.

482. The *Aurora*.

483. a. Photon torpedoes.
    b. In "A Piece of the Action," as a show of force against the Iotians.

484. Warp 14.1. ("That Which Survives")

485. In two episodes—"The Tholian Web" and "Elaan of Troyius" (the Dohlman's quarters were Uhura's; she gave them up).

486. "The Tholian Web."

487. "The *Enterprise* Incident."

488. Ion power.

489. McKinley Rocket Base.

490. "Bread and Circuses."

491. Kirk, James T. The entire crew of the ship, the *Constellation*, has been killed, with the exception of Captain Decker. See "The Doomsday Machine" for details.

492. "The *Enterprise* is our vessel . . . sailing out at sea."

493. The *Lexington* and the *Excaliber*.

494. Deck Eight. ("I, Mudd")

495. The U.S.S. *Intrepid*.

496. Matter/antimatter.

497. "Mirror, Mirror."

498. Warp 2. ("Friday's Child")

499. Atomic engines.

500. "The Naked Time."

501. The S.S. *Botany Bay;* a ship in the DY-100 class.

502. "The Man Trap."

503. "Shore Leave," "Tomorrow Is Yesterday."

504. Twenty.

505. A city in space.

506. To record the breakup of PSI 2000.

507. Deck Twelve, Section Three.

508. Four.

509. Deck Fourteen, Section Six.

510. A warning buoy (a square, multicolored rotating device).

511. Ion power.

512. a. The engineering room.
b. To seek out new life forms.

513. The *Enterprise*.

514. Seven.

515. c. a shuttlecraft. ("The *Galileo Seven*")

516. Twenty-four feet.

517. Twelve.

518. Bluejay 4. (His base is called Blackjack 1.)

519. The U.S.S. *Republic*.

520. "Court-Martial" and "The Immunity Syndrome."

521. The U.S.S. *Valiant*.

522. 100 years ago.

523. Five times.

524. Four and one-half hours.

525. 97.835 megatons.

526. The U.S.S. *Constellation*.

527. The *Galileo*.

528. The U.S.S. *Dierdre* and the U.S.S. *Carolina*.

529. The *Wodon*.

530. The U.S.S. *Exeter*.

531. The U.S.S. *Yorktown*.

532. Leaving. (That's the back of the shuttlecraft.)

533. The U.S.S. *Farragut*.

534. A routine annual check of the scientific expedition on Gamma Hydra IV.

535. Deck Five. ("Journey to Babel")

CHAPTER 10

```
++++++++++++++++++++++++++++++++++++++++
   ORGANIAN          196 - 262
++++++++++++++++++++++++++++++++++++++++
   VULCAN            170 - 195
++++++++++++++++++++++++++++++++++++++++
   TALOSIAN          144 - 169
++++++++++++++++++++++++++++++++++++++++
   HUMAN             117 - 143
++++++++++++++++++++++++++++++++++++++++
   ANDORIAN           91 - 116
++++++++++++++++++++++++++++++++++++++++
   ROMULAN            65 - 90
++++++++++++++++++++++++++++++++++++++++
   KLINGON            39 - 64
++++++++++++++++++++++++++++++++++++++++
   TRIBBLE            13 - 38
++++++++++++++++++++++++++++++++++++++++
   SLIME DEVIL         0 - 12
++++++++++++++++++++++++++++++++++++++++
```

ELECTRONIC FRIENDS AND ENEMIES (ROBOTS, ANDROIDS, COMPUTERS)

536. a. Tan Ru. ("The Changeling")

537. "The Ultimate Computer" (the M-5) and "I, Mudd" (Mudd's androids).

538. "A mass of conflicting impulses."

539. In August 2002.

540. Flint the Immortal (as a replacement for the M-4) and Dr. Daystrom (as a computer that would revolutionize space travel). ("Requiem for Methuselah" and "The Ultimate Computer")

541. The Hall of Audiences. ("The Return of the Archons")

542. "Code 1-2-3-Continuity. Abort Destruct Order."

543. Gary Seven.

544. Simply because they are, in M-5's words, "non-essential personnel."

545. "M" for "Multitronics," "5" for fifth in the series.

546. "The most ambitious computer complex ever created. Its purpose is to correlate all computer

activity of a starship . . . to provide the ultimate in vessel operation and control."

547. A negatron hydrocoil.

548. Norman #1.

549. "Please."

550. Stella. (This question is in this chapter because Mudd made a computerized nagging shrine of her. It will constantly criticize him until he says the magic words, "Shut *up*, Stella!")

551. Pure neutronium.

552. In the Guardian's own words, "I am both . . . and neither." ("The City on the Edge of Forever")

553. "Tomorrow Is Yesterday."

554. One.

555. No. But Kirk says she really doesn't need any. All she has to know is, "Touch the wrong line and you're dead."

556. No.

557. Four (Brown, Ruk, Andrea, and Korby).

558. The Old Ones. ("What Are Little Girls Made Of?")

559. Brown, or, more affectionately, Brownie.

560. "Pasteur of archaeological medicine."

CHAPTER 11

++
| ORGANIAN | 61 – 82 |
++
| VULCAN | 53 – 60 |
++
| TALOSIAN | 45 – 52 |
++
| HUMAN | 36 – 44 |
++
| ANDORIAN | 28 – 35 |
++
| ROMULAN | 20 – 27 |
++
| KLINGON | 12 – 19 |
++
| TRIBBLE | 4 – 11 |
++
| SLIME DEVIL | 0 – 3 |
++

Chapter Twelve
ALL HAILING FREQUENCIES OPEN . . .

561. d. "Kirk to Enterprise."

562. In "Tomorrow Is Yesterday," when it goes back in time to Earth.

563. Mars Toothpaste.

564. The Galactic Cultural Exchange Project.

565. The Book of the People.

566. Boxes.

567. Subspace B three-nine.

568. Three weeks.

569. The news report. (If you have a black-and-white TV, give yourself four mercy points for this question.)

570. It indicates trouble. But it also forbids the taking of any action by the receiver of the message.

571. Code 2.

572. To obtain mining rights on Capella IV.

573. A compressed binary, carrying many channels at once.

574. A place to sleep.

575. *War* (declared by the Klingons, those nasty devils).

576. Ship-to-surface. ("We'll be needing it for a while.")

577. "Under no circumstances approach planet." ("A Taste of Armageddon")

578. Decontamination of the planet Ariannus.

579. It means: destroy said planet in (given) hours (or minutes, or days, or whatever).

580. "Greetings and felicitations. Hip, Hip, Hurrah! Tally-ho!"

581. A laser beacon.

582. By subspace radio.

583. He "broke the rule of silence."

584. "No vessel under any condition, emergency or otherwise, is to visit Talos IV."

585. *Death.* ("The Menagerie")

586. "This is Balok, Commander of the Flagship Fesarius of the First Federation."

587. "You don't need all that subspace chatter."

588. Security Condition 3.

589. Every year.

590. A disaster call. It signals near or total disaster. ("The Trouble with Tribbles")

591. Subspace radio.

592. "This is Captain James T. Kirk, of the Starship *Enterprise*."

593. Standard radio, Morse Code.

594. A bell.

CHAPTER 12

```
++++++++++++++++++++++++++++++++++++++++++++++
    ORGANIAN              88 - 118
++++++++++++++++++++++++++++++++++++++++++++++
    VULCAN                76 - 87
++++++++++++++++++++++++++++++++++++++++++++++
    TALOSIAN              64 - 75
++++++++++++++++++++++++++++++++++++++++++++++
    HUMAN                 53 - 63
++++++++++++++++++++++++++++++++++++++++++++++
    ANDORIAN              41 - 52
++++++++++++++++++++++++++++++++++++++++++++++
    ROMULAN               29 - 40
++++++++++++++++++++++++++++++++++++++++++++++
    KLINGON               17 - 28
++++++++++++++++++++++++++++++++++++++++++++++
    TRIBBLE                5 - 16
++++++++++++++++++++++++++++++++++++++++++++++
    SLIME DEVIL            0 - 4
++++++++++++++++++++++++++++++++++++++++++++++
```

Chapter Thirteen
NUMBERS, LETTERS, AND SYMBOLS

595. This is from the episode "The Way to Eden." (You can tell by the landscape.) In the episode "The *Galileo Seven*," which was filmed before "Eden," the first *Galileo* was destroyed.

596. NCC-1701.

597. It would take Cyrano Jones 17.9 years to remove

every single tribble from space station K-7. ("The Trouble with Tribbles")

598. Well, "Assuming that one tribble with an average litter of ten producing a new generation every twelve hours over a period of three days, and taking into account the amount of grain in the container . . ." He eventually ends up with a nice round figure of one million, seven hundred and seventy-one thousand, five hundred and sixty-one tribbles.

599. I.S.S.

600. Star Fleet Order 104, Section B.

601. Thirteen.

602. "And the Children Shall Lead."

603. Seventy-three (Khan included).

604. About 200 years.

605. 12 percent under normal, and dropping steadily.

606. One.

607. Two.

608. Credits. ("The Trouble with Tribbles," "Mirror, Mirror")

609. Widin Dairy Farms.

610. Six hours.

611. It comes within one parsec.

612. 1,400 hours.

613. It goes down to −250° F.

614. Forty-seven.

615. Six credits.

616. Six. ("Mudd's Women")

617. The Onlies. "Grup" is a shortened form of "grown-up," but unfortunately the adults are long dead, while the children have aged very little in 300 years.

618. One month.

619. "Destination:
     Bureau of Penology, Stockholm, Eurasia–NE
     Classified Material—Do Not Open!"

620. Seven.

621. Nineteen.

622. 4,000; on Tarsus IV.

623. According to "Balance of Terror," those are the coordinates for the neutral zone.

624. Eleven.

625. Twenty.

626. 500 pounds.

627. He is 900 years too early. This is due to the fact that he uses a conventional light telescope. Since the *Enterprise* travels faster than light, it can get to Trelane's planet before the light rays of Earth can.

628. Fifty billion credits.

629. 200 years. (Golly!)

630. 4857932. (Did ya get it?)

631. Six o'clock.

632. Numbers 11 and 12.

633. United Federation of Planets.

634. For six years.

635. Once, on the primary (saucer-shaped) hull, above the large, curving serial number.

636. The Depression Era (1930s).

637. Chart 14A.

638. *About* 15,800 credits (we never get the exact figure).

639. 72° F.

640. 1992.

641. A code in the form of alien musical notes.

642. b. freedom.

643. 1968.

644. SE 197 547 230T.

CHAPTER 13

```
+++++++++++++++++++++++++++++++++++++++++++++++
   ORGANIAN                     159 - 212
+++++++++++++++++++++++++++++++++++++++++++++++
   VULCAN                       137 - 158
+++++++++++++++++++++++++++++++++++++++++++++++
   TALOSIAN                     116 - 136
+++++++++++++++++++++++++++++++++++++++++++++++
   HUMAN                         95 - 115
+++++++++++++++++++++++++++++++++++++++++++++++
   ANDORIAN                      74 - 94
+++++++++++++++++++++++++++++++++++++++++++++++
   ROMULAN                       53 - 73
+++++++++++++++++++++++++++++++++++++++++++++++
   KLINGON                       31 - 52
+++++++++++++++++++++++++++++++++++++++++++++++
   TRIBBLE                       10 - 30
+++++++++++++++++++++++++++++++++++++++++++++++
   SLIME DEVIL                    0 - 9
+++++++++++++++++++++++++++++++++++++++++++++++
```

Chapter Fourteen
WHO (OR WHAT) SAID THAT?

645. b. "We are One," the basic saying of the "space
     hippies" in "The Way to Eden."

646. Eymorg. ("Spock's Brain")

647. "Mind your own business, Mister Spock! I'm sick of your half-breed interference! Do you hear?"

648. Scotty, in "Mudd's Women."

649. "Do you think you might gather up all the cord and wire on board and lower us a pot of hot coffee?"

650. "You don't rank me and you don't have pointed ears."

651. "There was a warped baffle plate on the shield of their energy pile. I made it go away."

652. McCoy to Spock in "The Immunity Syndrome."

653. "Hail Hail fire and snow; call the Angel. We will go far away, for to see. Friendly Angel come to me."

654. "Better to rule in hell than serve in heaven."

655. Lieutenant Gary Mitchell. ("Where No Man Has Gone Before")

656. "Balance of Terror."

657. "Fool me once, shame on you; fool me twice, shame on me."

658. The Klingon says the *Enterprise* should be "hauled away as garbage."

659. c. "Plum," spoken by Nancy Crater.

660. "Let's get the hell out of here."

661. Regulan blood worms.

662. Scotty.

663. ". . . the lilies of the field. They toil not, neither do they spin."

664. "A swaggering, overbearing, tin-plated dictator with delusions of godhood!" He also compares him with a creature known as a "Denebian slime devil."

665. Rank Hath Its Privileges.

666. "Jimmy-boy." (!)

667. "The Squire of Gothos."

668. Anan 7.

669. "This Side of Paradise."

670. "This Side of Paradise."

671. "No Kill I."

672. Mudd's androids, when asked a question to which the answer is unknown or secret.

673. ". . . exciting . . ."

674. Kor's "Tell me about the dispersal of your Star Fleet."

675. ". . . a ram among the sheep."

676. "The City on the Edge of Forever."

677. "Any home port the ship makes will be somebody else's . . . not mine!"

678. "I shall certainly break your neck."

679. "Just before they [the Klingons] went into warp I transported the whole kit and kaboodle into their engine room . . . where they'll be no tribble at all."

680. "Day of the Dove." It is Kang's reaction to the situation that the alien being (the one that feeds on hatred) has put them in.

681. "Logic is little tweeting bird, chirping in meadow. Logic is pretty flowers, which smell *bad*. Are you sure your circuits are registering correctly? Your ears are *green*."

682. McCoy's "beads and rattles."

683. "They do not talk too much."

684. Zefrem Cochrane.

685. McCoy. ("Journey to Babel")

686. Gav the Tellarite's "There will be payment for your slander, Sarek." ("Journey to Babel")

687. Russia. ("Friday's Child")

688. c. "That hurts worse than the uniform." (Spock is trying to teach McCoy the Vulcan salute in "Journey to Babel.")

689. A dead man.

690. Luck.

691. A word used by midshipmen. It refers to a part that serves no useful purpose.

692. Scotty, in "Elaan of Troyius."

693. President Lincoln in "The Savage Curtain."

694. "Queen to King's Level One." (Used by Kirk as a password to get back to the *Enterprise* in "Whom Gods Destroy.")

695. "All Our Yesterdays" (Spock).

696. Klingonese. ("The Trouble with Tribbles")

697. Jupiter Eight Auto.

698. Actually, an iguana would be more precise. Remember when Charlie Evans turned a pretty yeoman into a lizard? That was Ms. Lawton. ("Charlie X")

699. T'Pau.

700. McCoy. ("Well, it's better than 'Hey, you!' ")

701. Nomad, the super robot, destroys them for being "imperfect biological units."

702. ". . . the ship's bowling alley at 1900 hours."

703. A personal log, or diary. Unfortunately, it also serves as a radio, so the Gorn is able to listen to and locate Kirk.

CHAPTER 14

```
++++++++++++++++++++++++++++++++++++++++++
   ORGANIAN            149 - 199
++++++++++++++++++++++++++++++++++++++++++
   VULCAN              129 - 148
++++++++++++++++++++++++++++++++++++++++++
   TALOSIAN            109 - 128
++++++++++++++++++++++++++++++++++++++++++
   HUMAN                89 - 108
++++++++++++++++++++++++++++++++++++++++++
   ANDORIAN             69 - 88
++++++++++++++++++++++++++++++++++++++++++
   ROMULAN              49 - 68
++++++++++++++++++++++++++++++++++++++++++
   KLINGON              29 - 48
++++++++++++++++++++++++++++++++++++++++++
   TRIBBLE               9 - 28
++++++++++++++++++++++++++++++++++++++++++
   SLIME DEVIL           0 - 8
++++++++++++++++++++++++++++++++++++++++++
```

I hope you've been keeping track of your acquired gradients 'cause this is it—the totals score chart for the entire book.

The shock of finding out how much you didn't know about Trek is over. It's time to get up and wildly run around the house shouting "I did it! I did it!" If that's not your style you can just sink into your comfy chair and quietly contemplate the universe you just explored.

Hopefully your total score shows that you are at least an Andorian. If you did better than that, good for you. But if you really flubbed—don't worry—some of my best friends are Denebian Slime Devils.

Peace and long life to you all.

-TOTALS-

+++
| ORGANIAN | 1921 - 2562 |
+++
| VULCAN | 1665 - 1920 |
+++
| TALOSIAN | 1409 - 1664 |
+++
| HUMAN | 1152 - 1408 |
+++
| ANDORIAN | 896 - 1151 |
+++
| ROMULAN | 640 - 895 |
+++
| KLINGON | 384 - 639 |
+++
| TRIBBLE | 128 - 383 |
+++
| SLIME DEVIL | 0 - 127 |
+++